D1255103

Love Ordained

by Tara Taffera

Fiction and Literature: Inspirational Christian Romance

ISBN: 978-1-952661-63-1

Chapter 1

Four months after the accident

Gina opened the door of her ranch-style home and noticed some of the stucco had started to peel. Just another thing she would have to ignore. She walked up the steps with her one bag of groceries and looked at the wreath that hung on the door. The word welcome, along with the singing birds and flowers that appeared on the wreath Helena had bought her, left an impression for those who saw it that this was a warm and welcoming house full of cheer. That was once true—but not anymore. Now it only reminded her of the heartache she was feeling. She opened the door quickly as she was still incapable to think of Alex and Teresa for more than a few minutes at a time.

She turned on the light and was greeted by darkness. That's funny. She swore Alex had changed the bulb before he ... She couldn't even finish the sentence. It would have to stay that way. Gina felt so weak that something like going to the drawer to find a light bulb, then climbing on a chair to change it, just seemed unbearable. To her, every task seemed like an insurmountable challenge that she simply didn't have the energy to even attempt, let alone try and fail. On most days she felt like the carpets were made of quick sand and if she lingered too long they would swallow her whole. Though many times she wished they would.

She walked in the kitchen and flipped the switch, but all she saw was darkness. She looked at the three piles of mail still on the table—all of which were increasing in size. God only knew where that power bill was. Gina's father had been paying them for her but the last time he was here he said she had to start doing it herself. He had shown her where everything was, and made it seem so easy. Her eyes then fell on the coffee table where her Bible lay. How long had it been since she leafed through its pages—something she used to do every day without even thinking.

Pushing those thoughts away, she pulled the bottle of cabernet that she just bought from Publix along with a loaf of bread, a jar of peanut butter, a bottle of jelly and a bag of pretzels out of the grocery bag.

About one month after the accident she decided to buy some of the food she used to enjoy. She walked down one of the supermarket aisles in search of what she wanted with plans of making a quick escape. But when she unknowingly strolled up the baby food aisle and saw the items she used to buy for Teresa she broke down in tears. Once she started crying, the tears came fast and furious and a Winn Dixie employee had to help her to the car. After that, she drove the few extra miles to Publix and stuck to buying just a few things.

As she looked at the peanut butter and jelly, she suddenly craved a piece of Helena's homemade baklava. Gina had been having all kinds of sweet cravings lately. She knew that would happen but for now she would have to be happy with her peanut butter sandwich. The sound of the doorbell interrupted her thoughts. It was probably Elizabeth. Who else could it be? She hadn't spoken to Alex's parents, John and Helena, sister Anna and brother Christian since the accident. Maybe it was Pastor Tom, someone she really didn't want to face—especially with the bottle of wine on the table.

She really hoped it was Elizabeth, her friend since grade school, and hoped she could tell her she was fine then maybe she would be left alone for a few more days. Elizabeth was like Gina's parents, in that she kept checking up on her to make sure she was okay. But since her parents lived two hours away from Gina's house in Tarpon Springs, Florida, it was Elizabeth who checked in on her a few times a week. And if she didn't answer the door her friend was persistent. She would bang away for an hour, if that's what it took for Gina to show herself. But, tonight she wanted to get it over with so she opened it after the first knock. Maybe Elizabeth would go through these bills, or better yet do it for her, and find that stupid envelope from the power company. She adjusted the large oversized sweatshirt she was wearing so it looked extra bulky.

"Hi Eliza—" she said.

But it wasn't her best friend, it was the two people in the world that, although they loved her dearly, were the last ones she wanted to see right now.

"Mom, Dad. What are you doing here?"

Gina's mother Maria walked in the darkened house first. Her father Sal followed behind and immediately went for the light switch. She heard him mutter under his breath as he stomped over to flip the switch to the kitchen. When that didn't work, he looked at the thermostat, and she could see the flaming red start to show up on his cheeks.

"Come on, Gina! How hard is it to pay a couple of lousy bills?"

Before she could answer, not that she would have anyway, her mother jumped in.

"Sal, please," her mother said.

"Please, what? I know she's going through a lot but paying these wouldn't be that hard if she hadn't relied on Alex to do all of this."

Maria just sighed as she sat down and started to go through it all.

She looked at her mother with relief knowing she would take care of everything. It wasn't always like this. Yes, Alex took care of the bills, but Gina was as independent and capable as they came. It was one of the things Alex always told her he loved about her. But everything changed after he died. She didn't have the strength to do any of it.

"Oh, no you don't," Sal yelled, knocking Gina back to the present. "How is she ever going to take care of herself if everyone keeps doing things for her? She needs to get it together!"

After months of sitting silent as her father droned on about how she needed to move on and take control of her life, something in her snapped.

"What's wrong with you helping me out?" she

screamed. "I just lost my husband and daughter."

"You lost them four months ago," he screamed back.

"Oh, sorry, Dad. So, tell me. How long can I grieve? Should I have been done in two months, three? I guess I didn't receive my copy of the grieving widow's handbook. Why don't you run out and buy me a copy so I know how I should act."

"Oh, don't give me that 'woe is me' sad song. That's all I've been hearing from you. I know this has been hard, Gina. It's hard for us too," then his tone became slightly softer. "But you have to take responsibility. If Teresa were here you'd have to do all these things to take care of her. Would you let her exist on peanut butter and jelly sandwiches?"

"It doesn't matter because Teresa isn't here, is she?" she screamed in a boom that made her earlier outburst seem subdued.

"No, she isn't," her Dad yelled taking her cue. "And you have to start dealing with that like the rest of us are. We won't be back again until you start taking care of yourself. We won't keep doing it for you."

He grabbed Mom's hand and led her out the door and slammed it behind him. She saw her mother look back through the window and knew that even though she would want to help she was too weak to stand up to her hot-tempered Italian husband.

~

Gina woke from her cabernet-induced slumber by the sound of the doorbell. She looked outside trying to figure out if it was the sun rising or setting. Then she remembered her parents left a few hours ago.

Gina opened the door, and although she was not

fully awake, the person standing there made her eyes widen instantly.

"Helena," was all she could manage. Though she tried to will her lips open, her mouth wouldn't cooperate.

Gina ran her fingers through her hair in an attempt to straighten her greasy locks that hadn't been washed in at least four days, though she had lost all track of time lately.

"How are, y--?"

"I'm only here to tell you that some of your things are at our house and if you don't come over by Friday to pick them up it's all going in the trash. We'll leave it on the stoop for you. Don't bother knocking. Just take it and go." Then she turned and left.

There were a lot of things Gina would have loved to say. How is the family? Why have you stopped inviting me over each Sunday for the weekly dinner? Why does no one in the family call me or text me or answer me when I reach out to them? Or better yet: Why have I been banished from the family I have loved so much for almost eight years? Why are you punishing me like this? But she couldn't find the words. She wanted to go inside and take a long swallow of her cabernet, though deep down she knew she shouldn't be drinking it, but she couldn't move. When her legs finally unglued themselves from her cement steps, Helena turned toward her.

"By the way, I heard about your breakdown in Winn Dixie. I really hope you're seeing someone who can help you with that."

Just as Gina thought Helena's heart might be melting slightly. That she was ready to let Gina back in her heart, she stomped on it once more.

"I'd really hate for that to happen again and for you to embarrass the family even further."

Chapter 2

Seven years before the accident

"Do you think they'll like me?" Gina asked Alex for the hundredth time as they made the hour-long drive from their college campus at the University of Tampa to Alex's family's house.

What would they think when they met her? It had taken her more than two hours to choose an outfit for a simple lunch. She would later learn that nothing with Alex's family was simple.

"They'll love you," he said while gazing at her appreciatively.

"By the way, you look wonderful."

She was now happy with the outfit she chose: a pair of khaki slacks and a red short-sleeved blouse. Everyone always told her that red was her color, especially Alex.

He always put her at ease. Although they had been seeing each other for more than six months, she always felt as if she had just met him the week before. With every compliment he gave her, which he doled out frequently, she could feel her face flush. Although she was dark complected, you could always tell when she blushed and Alex constantly teased her about it. That's one of the things she loved so much about him—that they could just goof around, tease each other—she laughed so much with Alex. She was just so comfortable with him, even right from the day they met. A part of her was hoping it would be that way with his family as well.

"Now, who's going to be there again?"

"Well, there's my Dad."

"John."

"Right," Alex confirmed.

"And his brothers, George and Andrew, with their wives, Lydia and Angela."

"I'm impressed. Have you been taking notes then memorizing them at night when you should be studying for exams?"

"No, but I want to make sure I have it straight. I'm not used to having so much family to keep track of."

"You'll be fine."

"I know all of the men in your family are cops but you're not going to sneak away and talk shop all night, are you? You better not leave me too long."

"Well, I may have to run just a few scenarios by them for my criminal justice classes. You do want me to be an amazing cop like them one day, right?"

She gave him a side eye, and could see him smiling, though he was trying not to. She swatted him playfully.

"Seriously, promise not to leave me too long."

"I'm kidding. I'll be by your side all day, of course. But if I happen to get pulled away, you can always talk to Anna and Christian. They're really excited to meet you."

"I'm excited to meet your brother and sister too. Are you sure they will like me?"

"Gina, I've never seen you so nervous. Relax," he said while caressing her arm then pulled into the driveway.

~

As Gina helped Helena clear the dishes, she laughed at herself silently for being on edge. The day could not have gone better.

"So, Gina. You said your parents live in Ocala?"

"That's right," Gina answered nervously as she wondered if she was about to be subjected to a game of 20 questions.

"You must miss them while you're away at school."

"I do. But, they come to visit sometimes since it's only an hour and a half away."

"And Alex said you're an only child?"

"That's right."

"Did you miss not having any siblings?"

"A little. I always thought it would be great to be part of a big family, and to always have people around. But my parents are the best. I couldn't have asked for a better family."

"I'd love to meet them someday. But, I'm sure I will. I have a feeling I'll be seeing a lot of you."

Gina smiled, and Helena continued with her questions, even though she suspected she already knew some of the answers. Alex admitted to her that his mother had been asking quite a lot about Gina.

"So, Alex tells me you are studying business? How do you like it?"

"I love it. I have dreams of starting my own company one day. I'm not sure what yet—something to do with planning events, and I think having that business background will really help me."

"You must be really organized."

"I definitely am but I think it's a plus with my future plans."

"So, what about a family?"

Wow, she didn't waste any time.

"Oh, I definitely want a family one day and that's why I think this is a perfect career choice for me. It's something I can do a lot of from home while still raising children."

"It sounds like you have some amazing dreams. You must stay really busy."

"I do. But I like it that way."

"I'm sorry about all the questions. How about dessert? I hope you like baklava."

"I love it. Alex told me yours is the best in town."

"Hmmph. It's the best anywhere. Wait until you try all the other things I make. I'm going to work on fattening you up a bit," she said as her large brown eyes scanned Gina's slender frame.

"Oh, no," Gina said. "I don't need any help in that department."

Gina wouldn't describe herself as skinny, though many people told her she was. At 5 feet, 8 inches tall she was a size 8 and strived to be a 6 but her body wouldn't cooperate.

"Gina, are you talking about your weight?" asked Alex as he walked into the room with Christian and draped his arm comfortably around her shoulder. "I think you're perfect."

"Oh Lord, enough with the mushiness already," Christian said, while walking over to his mother and giving her a wink.

"What, you can't handle it, Bro? You're just mad because Gina just beat you in Phase 10—something no one ever does."

"Oh, believe me there will be a rematch and I will reclaim my crown."

"You better start practicing then because I never lose," Gina teased back.

"Oh, really now," he said while walking toward her and giving her a friendly nudge. You just wait."

Helena watched the exchange, happy that Gina fit in so well, and watched as Alex leaned over and gave Gina a kiss on her cheek. "Come on you lovebirds. Let's have Gina test my baklava."

Gina sat in the car nestled against Alex as they made the one-hour drive back to college.

"What are you so happy about?"

"I love your family, and I think they like me too."

"They do, especially my mother. I didn't want to make you more nervous, but she's very protective of us kids. Thankfully, I can tell she approved."

Chapter 3

The day of the accident

Gina looked at herself in the mirror, admired her new mauve colored lipstick and knew Alex would love it. She chose a simple outfit for their date at home tonight. Her skinny jeans that she had to admit hugged her frame in all the right places. And a red blouse, Alex's favorite color, and the hue that everyone always told her complemented her black hair nicely. Today her thick mane was pulled back in a slick ponytail.

She headed downstairs to check her sauce that had been cooking slowly on the stove for hours. She has been so busy with everything that comes along with having an almost two-year old that she hadn't made her famous sauce for months. Alex would be thrilled to know that is what she cooked tonight for their date.

Gina looked at her watch wondering where Alex was. He should have been home with Teresa by now as he was scheduled to pick her up from daycare more than an hour ago then drop her off at Elizabeth's for the night. She checked her phone—no texts or calls. Before worry had a chance to set in, she decided to keep herself busy checking on the sauce and finishing dinner. She was so looking forward to having some time with Alex alone. She loved her daughter but it's hard to have a conversation with constant interruptions from her precarious little girl. This would allow them to have some uninterrupted conversations. She had been thinking about opening her event planning business in the next few years when Teresa went to school—and she was excited to fill Alex in on some of her plans. But she also knew she would be counting the minutes until she saw Teresa again in the morning.

Another half hour had passed. She picked up her phone to text Alex but it started ringing and the caller ID said Rocco, Alex's friend, and partner on the force.

"Hi, Rocco."

"Gina, there's been an accident with Alex and Teresa you need to get to St. Ambrose hospital right away."

Before she could ask anything else, he hung up. She grabbed her keys on the kitchen table, spotted the sauce on the burner, turned it off and ran out the door. The hospital was only a ten-minute ride and when she got in the car she immediately started praying.

"Dear Lord, please have your angels watch over Teresa and Alex right now and keep them safe. I don't know what happened Lord, but you do so please watch over my family."

She pulled in a parking space and started running toward the emergency room, hoping they would be able to help her though she didn't even know if that's where they would be. "Dear Lord, please help me."

When she got to the desk, she opened her mouth to give her last name to the woman working there and immediately started crying.

"Gina."

She turned around to see Rocco. "What happened?"

"Come with me and I will take you to them."

She followed, but not before she saw the look of sympathy in the woman's eyes as she left.

Rocco guided her down the hospital's hallway then pulled her inside a vacant room smelling of disinfectant and death. She was crying freely now and for the first time she noticed the redness in his eyes.

"Rocco."

"It's bad, Gina. They were traveling on highway 19 from the daycare center when a driver ran a red light and hit them at full speed."

"Oh my God."

"An ambulance came to the scene right away. I was on duty and heard the call come in and headed right over there."

"Are they?"

"Gina. I am so sorry but the impact was just too much for a little girl ..."

This wasn't happening. She screamed and fell to the floor in tears. She heard someone enter the room and was relieved to see it was Helena. She expected her to come over and pull her into her arms but she just looked at Gina with contempt.

"Look what you've done."

Rocco looked at the two women staring at each other. One with hate, the other with confusion and despair. Thankfully a doctor walked into the room to break the tension, if that was even possible given the circumstances. He looked at Gina, "Are you Alex's wife?"

"Yes."

"And I am his mother," Helena interjected.

"Then I will brief you both. But first let me tell you how terribly sorry I am about your daughter. We did everything we could. Your husband's condition is very grave. The impact from the other car was severe, and although he was wearing his seatbelt, he suffered severe trauma to his head."

"Can I see him?"

"Yes, he has been asking for you. I know this a sensitive subject, and I'm not going to tell you what to do, but he is very anxious to hear about his daughter."

"I'm not going to give him that burden right now," Gina said, while looking straight in Helena's eyes, and trying to wipe the tears from her own. She didn't want Alex to know what a mess she was. She wanted to be strong for him like he always was for her.

The doctor seemed to breathe a sigh of relief. "I'm glad you came to that conclusion as I believe it is the best course of action."

Helena's stare deepened and was filled with additional contempt aimed at Gina.

"Rocco. Helena. I would like to pray before I go see Alex. Will you join me?" She held out her hands, and while Rocco walked right into them, Helena turned and left the room.

~

"How is Teresa?" Alex asked in a barely audible tone.

Just a few minutes after Gina was given the worst news of her life, that her daughter was dead, she was sitting by Alex in a drab hospital room. The doctor said she only had a few minutes with her husband as he was slipping in and out of consciousness.

"Gina," he said as he squeezed her hand.

"Alex." She didn't want to cry for him. She wanted to be strong, but she couldn't even say his simple name without crying again.

"What's wrong? Tell me the truth, Gina."

He could barely get the words out, Gina noticed. He was so weak, a trait completely unfamiliar to her husband who never exuded anything but strength and confidence. Whenever she thought of him on the job, she always remembered one particular day when she stopped by to surprise him—it was their anniversary and she wanted to take him on a picnic. She heard his voice, strong, yet somehow slightly gentle at the same time, telling a fellow officer to go back and talk to one of the suspects they had in custody. Alex was convinced this man was guilty and he was giving the officer hints at how to squeeze the truth out of the thug. That was always Alex's way—he was thought of by all the other cops as one to be feared but also as one of the few they could trust.

"I'm just so worried about you."

"I'll be fine. I'm not leaving my girls."

Gina loved when Alex referred to her and Teresa in this way.

"Where's Teresa? Is she going to be okay?"

Gina watched the monitor, not that she really knew what any of it meant, but she didn't want to get him more upset, and she knew she may only have a few more minutes with him. She doesn't know how she would go on--and she's healthy. The news would kill

Alex.

"Gina. Tell me."

"She's going to be okay."

"Really?"

"Yes. She has a lot of healing to do but she'll come through it. You have to get better too. I can't take care of her all by myself. You know how much we need you."

Alex smiled and then closed his eyes, but somehow Gina knew he was gone. When she tugged at his hand and felt no movement, she simply rested her head on his chest for the last time.

~

Gina leaned against the wall of the hospital room hallway and listened to her father-in-law talk to the cop who was investigating the car crash.

"The safety belt kept her in her car seat," said the officer who paused not wanting to go on but at the same time wanting to get this unbearable conversation over with. "But the impact was too severe. She died instantly. They found her in the vehicle with her eyes open clutching her teddy bear."

For Gina, it was more than she could take. She crumpled to the floor, like a pile of clothes cast aside, with her hands clutching her head as if she were willing her brain to keep these horrific images out. But all she could picture was Teresa sitting in her car seat with the gift Gina bought for her first birthday. Teresa took Mr. Bear everywhere she went but now both her husband and daughter were gone.

"Gina. Please look at me," John said suddenly.

"Gina," he said again. "I have something for you."

She moved her hands away from her head long

enough to see John holding the plush animal out to her.

"I thought you might want to have this."

~

Gina sat alone in the hospital chapel. Alex was gone. In the past 12 hours her world had changed completely. Before Rocco's call, she had a family and felt more love than most people dream of. Now, she sat alone. She called her parents a few hours ago and they were on their way. But already her guilt was setting in. She knew she hadn't talked to them as much as she used to, as she got caught up in everything that was the Andros family. How could she not? Every family member was in a ten-mile radius while her parents were a few hours drive away.

She put her head in her hands and did the only thing she knew how to do.

"God, I don't understand your plan. I know you didn't bring this tragedy, but it's hard to remember that now. It's hard to think that somehow all of this sadness and anger is part of your will. Please show yourself to me, Lord. Show me how I am ever going to survive this?"

Gina often heard the voice of God. It calmed her, and it was something others envied. Today there was silence.

"Gina."

"Mom. Dad," then the tears came again, and she ran into their arms.

"We are so sorry, Gina. We are here for you. But why are you all alone?" Where is the rest of the family?"

"I haven't really seen them since everything happened."

Sal gave Maria an I told you so look.

"Well, we're here now. What do you need?" asked her mother, now in her usual go-mode.

"I don't know. I signed the papers, I guess there is nothing else to do here."

"Come on, Gina. We've got you."

Her mother guided Gina up from the pew with Sal trailing behind.

Chapter 4

"Gina, would you like me to call Helena to find out if they started making arrangements for the funeral?" her mother asked.

"Sure, Mom."

"Great, while I take care of that why don't you go lie down and we can talk about it when you get up."

"I am really tired … thank you."

"You're welcome. I know it doesn't feel like it now but God has you in the palm of his hand and he will get you through this. All of us."

The tears welled up yet again. Gina let them fall while she walked to the couch then cried herself to sleep.

~

Gina walked into the kitchen where her parents were talking in hushed voices.

"Mom. What did they say about the service?"

Maria gave Sal a knowing glance before answering.

"Gina, you know this is hard on everyone, right?"

"And?"

"Helena is handling all the arrangements and will email you the details."

"That's it?"

"I'm sorry, Gina."

"It's okay. I'll call Anna or Christian later. I am sure they have tried to get in touch with me. I haven't even looked at my phone since …"

Her father interrupted. "Gina, I think you should give them all some time. We're here and we will help you through this."

"Thanks, Dad. I love you."

"I love you too, G."

The house was so quiet. Gina tried to remember where her parents went—something about running an errand and telling her to sleep. It seemed that was her mother's answer for everything these past few days, though she found it almost impossible to do so.

Gina looked at her phone and saw 10 texts waiting to be read. She took a quick look and saw two from Elizabeth, one from each of three of her friends from college (Elizabeth must have told them) she guessed. But none from Christian or Anna. She checked them all again just to be sure, but there was nothing. The tears came freely again and continued until she fell asleep where she lay on the couch, the exhaustion of the past 48 hours finally hitting her.

~

"Sal, I have a bad feeling about the Andros'."

"So do I. Gina has been on Helena's good side all these years, but I think that has all changed. I only hope our daughter can make it through."

"She is going to be devastated. That family is

everything to her. Did you see her face when she found out no one from that family had called her?"

"Yes. It broke my heart but I am also filled with so much anger. At God. At Helena for cutting Gina out of planning her own husband's memorial."

"I know," Maria said as she took his hand that wasn't on the steering wheel. "All we can do is believe that her faith somehow brings her through this. He has gotten us through things before—we can't give up on Him now."

Gina awoke to the sound of a car driving away. She opened the door to see a mountain of food on her porch—way too much for one person. She couldn't even think about eating without her stomach turning into knots. Even the sight of her favorites like chocolate chip muffins, a pan of lasagna and more things she didn't even want to think about. Gina brought it inside and left it on the counter then went right back to the couch and pulled the blanket over her head while breathing in the scent of Alex and Teresa.

~

Maria and Sal let themselves in the house, and all the while Gina never woke up from where she was sleeping on the couch. Maria let her rest and started putting away all the food still sitting on the kitchen table. Gina's phone was there, and Maria picked it up to see if Christian or Anna had texted, praying for Gina's sake that they had. Nothing. It was just more texts from her college roommates, Elizabeth of course, and a few neighbors. And, a text from her pastor since she hadn't been returning his calls. "Well, at least we know who really cares about her now."

She clicked on the Gmail link and found a ton of

emails, including one from Helena, and Maria opened it.

"Gina, I wanted to let you know the funeral will be held Wed morning at 10 a.m. at St. Anthony's Church. After, mourners who so wish will come to our home. People will expect to see you there."

"Sal. I can't believe it. Look at this. She didn't even have the nerve to discuss any of this with Gina and she is not even having it at the church Alex and Gina attended. And then she says people will expect you to be there. Where the hell else would she be?"

Sal looked at his wife who never uttered a foul word.

"Maria. What do you want me to do?"

"I can't believe this is happening. I mean this whole situation would take months to get over in the first place and then that woman makes it worse by cutting her out of her life!"

~

Gina lay on the couch listening to her mother. She truly couldn't believe what she was hearing. It simply wasn't true. There was no way Helena would cut her out like that. And even if she wanted to, Gina knew there was no way Christian and Anna would let that happen. She got up to get her phone, startling her mother.

"Gina," her mother stuttered knowing she heard the earlier conversation but pretended it didn't happen.

"Mom, I heard what you said but there is no way it's true. I'm calling Anna," then grabbed her phone and walked up the stairs.

~

Anna sat at the large mahogany table at her

mother's house with her father and Christian when she heard the phone ring and saw the caller ID. She hit decline and glanced at her mother. Anna was sure her mother knew it was Gina, but pretended the phone never rang and continued the conversation.

"Okay, Mom, I think we have all the details together. Christian and I are going to the funeral home to finalize the details." She walked over and gave her a faint kiss on the cheek. "See you tomorrow."

"If I live that long," Helena muttered under her breath.

~

As soon as Anna and Christian were in the car, Anna pulled her phone out of her purse to call Gina.

"Anna, who are you calling?"

"Come on, Christian. I have to call her."

"You can't."

"Yes, I can she is like my own sister. Think of how you and I feel right now. I can't even imagine what she is going through."

"Anna, you know how much I loved Gina."

Anna cut him off. "Excuse me. Loved?"

"Whatever. We can't. She's our mother. We aren't going against her right now."

"So, we're supposed to go the funeral and ignore her? Refuse all her calls? The woman who we saw at least three times a week before this. The woman who you were super close to. You hung out with them all the time. How can you do this to her?"

"It will be hard but it's what we have to do."

"I can't do it, Christian."

"It's your funeral."

Anna just glared at him while she tucked the phone

back in her purse.

~

"Gina. Come on have something. I heated up some lasagna. You have to eat."

"I can't," she said as she poured herself a glass of wine.

"So, you're going to drown your sorrows? Do you really think that is the best way to cope with this?"

"I don't know, Mom. I mean really. How in the world do I get through this?"

Her Dad tried to ease the tension, which was often his role with the two women in his life.

"Gina. Come on. At least sit with us as we eat. Have a little bit."

She sat down, grabbed the smallest piece she could find, and picked at it as she drank her full glass of merlot. The phone rang but they let it go. The machine came on and the caller left a message.

"This is a reminder from Pediatric Associates that Teresa Andros has an appointment Thursday morning at 9 a.m."

Gina dropped her fork, picked up her wine and walked up the stairs.

~

Maria sat at the table crying and Sal could not console her. "I miss them too you know. I don't know how I am going to get us all through this."

"You don't have to, Maria. This is going to be a long road for all of us. We just have to be there for her. And each other," then he pulled his wife into his arms.

~

Anna and Christian had just left the funeral home when his phone rang. Now it was his turn to look at the caller ID. But he didn't ignore it like Anna did.

"Hi, Gina."

"Christian." She was glad but surprised he picked up. "How are you all doing? I'm surprised I haven't heard from any of you. I called Anna but she didn't answer."

"Well, sorry we are a little busy planning the funeral for our brother and niece."

He knew immediately she had started crying but he couldn't stop.

"Listen, Gina. My Mom emailed you about the funeral. We will see you then. Our family just needs space right now."

"I thought I was family."

He hung up without responding.

"Christian, I can't believe you did that. This is just too much. It's like we lost everyone in a day. She was part of us too you know."

"You need to get on board, Anna. We have to stick with Mom right now."

She didn't respond but wondered when two deaths in the family was a time to take sides. But she didn't have the time or energy to fight this battle.

Inside though, Christian was questioning his decision and tried not to think about how much he cared about Gina and what he was doing to her. He remembered when they hung out all the time starting early on in Alex and Gina's relationship.

~

Alex and Gina were sitting at Anna's house with Christian. It had only been three months since the two had been dating but they spent a lot of their time with Alex's siblings as Gina loved them almost as much as

Alex. And she knew the feeling was mutual.

Christian got up from his chair and snuggled right up to Gina and put his arm around her.

"So, when are you going to leave this guy and go out with the better brother?"

"I didn't know you two had another brother?"

"Real funny," Christian said.

"What's wrong, Bro? You aren't used to the chicks ignoring you huh?"

"Wait, when did I become a chick?"

"Sorry, babe. Christian, what I meant to say was you aren't used to the most beautiful, sweetest women ignoring you?"

"Much better," she said as the two met for a tender kiss.

"Oh, please. Take it somewhere else," Christian muttered.

"See, what did I say? Bitter."

Chapter 5

Gina sat on her bed wishing she had snuck the bottle of wine up to her room as she finished the glass long ago but refused to go back downstairs and have to talk to her parents. She knew they meant well but she wanted to be alone.

"You don't need that Gina. You need Me."

Gina ignored the voice and pulled the covers over her head.

~

Maria watched her daughter enter the kitchen the next morning in her black dress and matching heels and wished all of this was a horrible dream. How could it be they were about to bury Gina's husband and daughter.

"Come sit and eat something before we go."

"I can't, Mom. I already feel like I'm going to be sick."

"Then will you do something for me, Gina. Will you let me pray for you before we leave?"

She nodded, and her mother took her hand.

"Dear Lord, this is going to be the hardest day. We ask that you be with all of us and help us through it. Let Gina know you are with her and you will carry her through today and every day as she struggles with this tremendous loss. In your name we pray. Amen."

She opened her eyes and met Gina's that were full of tears.

~

Maria and Sal stood on each side of their daughter and held her hand. Sal stood up straight, took a breath, nodded to his wife then they both led Gina down the aisle. Sal looked at the Andros clan in the front row and slid into the pew behind them.

They all sat like frozen figures. Even when Gina's hand reached out to touch Christian and Anna on the shoulders, no one stirred. While her mother grabbed Gina's hand and said a silent prayer, Gina wished for a glass of wine. Or a bottle of wine. Anything to take away this stabbing sensation in her gut.

~

Maria walked out of the restroom of the church after the funeral was over and faced Helena Andros. Before she could slither away, Maria grabbed her arm.

"How dare you treat my daughter like this? She doesn't deserve your silence. Your obvious hatred."

"Oh, I think she does," then plucked Maria's hand off her black blazer and walked staunchly out the door.

~

"It was a beautiful service," Maria said as they made their way home. "Don't you think, Gina?"

"Mom, please just leave me alone."

~

"Sal, I am so worried about her."

"I am too. Did you see the way she was treated today by that family? I could wring all their necks with my bare hands."

"I know, Sal, but we have to worry about Gina."

"That's what I'm doing, Maria. What is she going to do when we leave? She has no support system besides Elizabeth. Did you see the way they all shut her out today?"

"Of course, I did. Don't you think I feel the same? But we have to put our energy into our daughter. I'm going to check on her."

At the top of the stairs, Maria was led to go right to Teresa's room instead of left to the master bedroom. She found Gina in a ball clutching Mr. Bear, her tears staining the plush cream carpet. She looked up at her mother and uttered a word she hadn't said since she was little.

"Mommy."

Maria's tears, which she had kept at bay all day to stay strong for her daughter, came freely now. She lay down on the carpet next to Gina holding her close.

"Why are they treating me like this? Was this really my fault?"

"Listen to me. Don't you ever say that again! Do you hear me?"

She nodded and fell asleep in her mother's arms.

Chapter 6

"Mom. Dad. It's been two weeks. I think it's time for you to go home."

Maria and Sal looked at each other, silently telling the other they weren't so sure.

"Dad, you've shown me everything I need to handle the finances. You guys have been great but I think you have to get back to your lives and I have to figure out how to get out of bed every day without you making me."

"Gina."

"It was a joke, Mom. I promise I won't keep the covers over my head all day. I have Elizabeth to check on me too."

"I still don't think we can leave you yet. Not when you have such a small support system."

And there it was.

"Mom. They will come around. I'm a part of their family. They can't shut me out forever."

"I think you have to face that they may do just that,

Gina."

"Sal!"

"What? You know it's true, Maria. That family abandoned her. She lost her husband and child and they turned their back when things got hard."

"It's okay, Mom. He can say it. But I don't believe it. I believe God brought me into Alex's life. He gave us our sweet girl, and he gave me the brother and sister I never had. I'm not accepting that he is taking all of them away from me."

The tears pooled once again in her mother's eyes.

"I'm so proud of your faith, Gina. I just hope you are right."

"And you know the minute you need us we are right back here."

"I know."

~

She watched her parents pull away then went into the kitchen to pour herself a glass of wine. Just one to take the edge off and then she would start going through the pile of sympathy cards on the table. Her mother opened them all for her and gave her the cliff notes but Gina figured she should finally look at them too.

She reached up to the wine rack above the refrigerator and pulled down the last bottle. She was positive she had several more up there. So much for her mother having faith in her, though she couldn't blame her.

She sat down with her wine glass and rifled through the pile. Our deepest sympathies … May God fill you with his strength … Our prayers are with you …

She opened each one and read all the messages.

There were about 20 in this stack and she imagined more would be coming. It seemed every day someone else heard the news and sent her an email or a card. They all said a variation of that same vague message. "I am here if you need me … Let me know what I can do? I'm only a phone call away …"

What she really needed was another glass of wine.

Chapter 7

One month after the accident

"It does get easier, Gina," the woman was saying as she held Gina's wrist with her slightly withered hand that gave away her age. Gina never wanted to escape someone's touch so badly. Why won't she get her pasty fingers off her? Why doesn't she take her meaningless advice and give it to some other pathetic person in this group? Let's face it, the only reason Gina was here is so her parents would leave her alone and would think she was okay. She laughed sarcastically to herself. Okay. What did that even mean? When would that ever be true again?

She was relieved to find that the pasty hand was now removed from Gina and was consoling another woman talking to the group.

"I think of my husband every day. Even though he's been gone for two years," said the well-dressed female who appeared to be about Gina's age.

Maybe if Gina wasn't in this awful room with a group of people she couldn't wait to get away from, perhaps she and this woman could have been friends. But, no way was she going to hang out with someone who was going to tell her all the time about how it would get better. She was sick of hearing that from everyone else in her life. She just wanted to remember Alex and Teresa.

Gina looked up and saw everyone staring at her.

"Gina, are you ready?"

"For what?" she answered to Dr. Roberts, the female leader of this pathetic clan.

"To tell your story."

You've got to be kidding me.

"There's not much to tell. I lost my husband and daughter in a car accident a month ago. My family--the family that still speaks to me anyway thinks I should stop wallowing and get some help, that I should talk to some people in the same situation as me. But I don't think we are the same. I lost two people in my life—in one day! With that car accident my world fell apart."

The pasty hand touched her again.

"I know it seems that way now, but it will get better. The pain will ease. You will start to move on. I know you can't imagine it now but your husband wouldn't want you living like this."

Gina pulled her hand away but the woman didn't seem to be offended.

"You've got to lean on all of your family now," said Dr. Roberts, before Gina cut her off.

"Well, that's a little difficult since most of my so-called family blames me for the deaths and have disowned me. So, you see, I really am alone—and that's fine."

For the first time that night there was silence. She craved it for the last hour but now she couldn't' wait for someone to start whining about a dead loved one. Gina guessed she must have stunned them. She must have been the only one with family that had abandoned her.

"Listen, honey."

Here we go again.

"We'll be your family. There are others you can turn to."

Were these people for real? They act like this is happy hour at the local bar.

"She's right, sweetie," said another middle-aged much too-happy woman in the group. "Ruthann here helped me get through the loss of my husband and now she's one of my closest friends."

Everyone in the room started smiling and cooing at each other. Gina wanted to vomit—a feeling she felt a lot of lately. This group was just making it worse. Oh, God, now they were hugging. That's it. She jumped up and started shouting.

"How can you all be sitting here like this is one big night out with friends? Some of you lost a husband. Others lost a child. How dare you sit here acting like this?"

Pasty hand was trying to talk again but Gina wouldn't let her.

"Really, don't bother," and with that she ran out of the room to the restroom down the hallway. She barely made it into the stall before she vomited into the toilet.

~

Gina lie in her bed wondering why that support

group got to her so much. Her grief had never turned to nausea like it did today, which just made her curse those women all over again. She was never going back there. She didn't care how much her parents pushed her to. She wouldn't listen to Elizabeth either. There was no way she was going through that a second time--the faces staring at her waiting for her to share her feelings. The nausea started to rise from her belly again, and she sprinted for the bathroom. Damn those women.

~

Gina spent the rest of the day under the covers only emerging a few times to answer Elizabeth's texts and tell her she was okay. She just wanted to rest and be alone and pleaded for her to understand. Her friend acquiesced but not before telling Gina she would be there Saturday. Normally, that's when Gina would go get a glass of wine to calm her nerves but today the thought of one made her ill. What was going on with her?

~

Gina got up the next day and dressed, putting on a pair of jeans that were loose in the waist. I guess I'm not eating much. Maybe everything will be okay. Maybe it's not what I think. She then left the house to drive about an hour away to a Walgreens where she prayed fervently that she wouldn't run into anyone she knew.

~

She left the store with her purchase but was in no hurry to get home. Gina was now only another hour's drive to her parents' house. Should she go over there? If they didn't hear from her soon, they would come just come visit her. She may as well get it over with.

She pulled into the drive of her childhood home and immediately started to feel calmer. She loved everything about this house, from the brick façade to the exquisitely trimmed bushes and flowers that lined the front perimeter. Maybe everything would be okay after all. She would go have a nice dinner with her parents and then make the drive home, but she wondered whose car was in the driveway.

She tried the knob and was surprised to find the door was open so she walked in but no one heard her. She tried to be quiet so she could surprise her parents— she knew they would be thrilled to know she actually got dressed and made the trip there. That undoubtedly would put a stop to their worries. She paused when she heard a familiar voice—one she never wanted to hear again.

"I just wish she would open up to us," the woman was saying, and Gina knew it was Dr. Roberts, the leader of the grief group. "Most people in the group are dealing with so much hurt that they want to confide in others who have gone through similar situations— particularly, the women. But she won't. I guess she just isn't ready. But don't worry we will be there when she is. Sometimes it just takes a little longer for others. She will be okay with time."

Gina couldn't breathe but knew she had to get out of there. She gently nudged open the door, tiptoed out and ran out to her car and left, hoping no one knew she had ever arrived at all.

Chapter 8

Present Day—Four months after the accident

Sal and Maria had just finished grabbing a quick bite at the diner down the street from Gina's, and Sal was settling the bill.

"I want to go somewhere before we leave town."

"Maria, I told you we're not going back to Gina's. She has to figure out that she has to start doing things herself, starting with getting that pile of bills paid."

"Sal, stop! We're going to Helena and John's."

~

Sal pulled up in front of the Andros' sprawling home complete with columns greeting visitors as they walked up the steps.

"I never could figure this out. What, are they trying to tell the world they're Greek?"

Maria just rolled her eyes at her husband.

"No, seriously. I'm surprised they don't have an olive tree in the yard."

Maria swatted him on the arm then rang the

doorbell. They were greeted immediately by John Andros.

"Sal and Maria. What a surprise," then embraced the two into his six-foot frame.

"How's Gina? Is she okay?"

"Actually, she's not," Maria quickly interjected. "That's why we're here. Did you know she barely gets herself out of bed? That her diet consists mainly of peanut butter and jelly sandwiches. Because even in the grocery store everything she sees reminds her of what she's lost. Did you know she has a pile of bills because she can't even summon the energy to open—let alone pay them?"

"Maria, I had no idea. Come in."

She walked into the Andros' expansive living area which at her first cursory glance looked exactly as she remembered it. But as her eyes roamed the room, she noticed that while nothing new had been added there were a few noticeable omissions since she was last here before Alex and Teresa died. The rocker that Gina always sat in while she was pregnant was gone. She used to say it was the only chair that made her feel halfway comfortable. There was now a vacant space on the mantle where the vase that Gina bought Helena and John for their 35th wedding anniversary used to be. Gina had stressed out so much over what to get the couple for that special occasion and finally settled on the expensive Waterford vase. Gina spared no expense to get a silver plate added on which she had engraved the couple's wedding date along with: "To Helena and John with all our love. Alex and Gina."

But the most noticeable omission was the photo of Alex and Gina on their wedding day. In fact, every frame with Gina in it had been taken down.

"Listen, John," Sal started, but Maria interrupted.

"Why don't you or Helena ever go to check on Gina?"

Not even giving him a chance to answer, she continued.

"And what about Anna and Christian--Gina was so close to them."

"It's just hard, Maria."

Maria took a second to gain her composure.

"It's hard? Imagine what it's like for her living in that house with all those memories. Imagine what it's like to lose the two people who were most important to you."

"Believe me, Maria. I know what it's like."

She paused again and exhaled.

"I'm sorry. That was insensitive of me."

"I did go over there once when she called me. She wasn't in good shape, but I just figured it was only a month or so since the accident and she would get better as time passed."

"She called you?"

"Yes, she was hearing noises. You know how Gina is scared of her own shadow when she is alone. Anyway, she couldn't find the key to the gun safe, and just wanted to know where it was for peace of mind."

"That's all she would have needed," Sal muttered.

John was silent.

"John, please tell me you didn't give her access to it."

Again, silence was his affirmative answer.

"What were you thinking, John?" yelled Sal, jumping off the couch and pacing the hardwood floors.

"You're a cop. You see people in these kinds of situations every day and you see what kind of damage they do to themselves?"

"I'm sorry. I thought it would help her feel safe. She lived with a cop. It's not like she didn't know how to use a gun or that she didn't already know how to access it. I don't know why she couldn't find the key anyway, it was right where he always kept it in his closet."

"I can't believe she has a gun," said Maria to no one in particular as she paced around the room. "What if she ..?" She couldn't even finish the sentence.

John stopped her frantic movements by grabbing her softly with both his arms, as gently as a man of his stature could.

"You know that if I even thought that was a possibility, I never would have given her the key. The last thing I would want is to lose her too. With everything she was going through I just wanted to help her feel safe in that house without him."

Sal was anxious to put the thoughts of his only daughter, in a depressed state with a gun, out of his mind. At the same time, he cursed himself for not thinking of this earlier. Of course, there would be a gun in the house. His daughter was married to a cop. Obviously, no one was thinking clearly since the accident.

"Listen, John. That's not why we came to talk to you—though let me tell you I can't believe you did such a stupid thing. Gina really isn't doing well. We thought she would finally start to get her energy back to at least do some mundane tasks but she can't even manage those. We try as much as we can to check up on her but we're not close enough."

"Say no more. I'll go over. Thanks for letting me know," then he stood up awkwardly as if bringing the visit to a halt.

Helena appeared in the doorway, and Maria just stared. It had been four months since she last saw Alex's mother at the funeral but she was finally showing her 70 years. She still looked perfect and proper with her freshly painted nails that were always the same cocoa color to her hair that was tied tightly in the same perfect bun. But her hair, though still black, was not a natural tone anymore, it had been dyed to hide her gray. And when you looked below her black-lined lids you could see the circles and fine lines that had finally made their mark.

"Thanks for talking to us, John," Sal said as he shook his hand.

"Helena," he said while nodding, then made his way toward the door.

"Hello, Helena," said Maria, making no moves toward following her husband.

Helena turned toward the living room.

"You're not going to say anything? You're going to act like we're not even here?"

Helena kept moving and gave John's beige windbreaker that was thrown over the sofa's arm a disapproving look. She picked it up, but before putting it away took the time to flick a speck of non-existent dust from the coffee table. She turned back toward the front door to usher them out but Maria couldn't leave without letting Helena know how much she had hurt her daughter.

"I knew it was you--the one who turned everyone against my daughter. John, Christian, Anna."

"Maria, please," said John.

"Please what? Are you still going to check on Gina now that your wife knows about it?"

John's silence and Helena's deafening stare was all the answer Maria needed.

"I just don't get it. What did she do? Gina thought of you as her family. Hell, Helena, she thought of you as a second mother. Why are you doing this to her? She needs you!"

Helena moved forward and matter-of-factly closed the door in the Galliano's faces.

~

Helena didn't yell or hurl accusations or questions when she turned toward John. She simply walked past him and up the stairs. Later he would have to explain what happened, apologize for letting them in, but for now he took in the calm before the storm that was his wife for the past 37 years. It was pretty simple with her—you were on her side or out in the cold.

~

"Have you forgotten him already? Do you not remember her smile? Her cute little laugh? The way Alex used to pick her up and carry her on his strong shoulders?"

Helena, who had just emerged from her bedroom after two hours, was now wearing a velour sweat suit, though she was still perfectly made up. The outfit was one many women would wear on a shopping trip though Helena would never leave the confines of her house in that attire.

John hadn't forgotten Alex—his first born who he thought of every time he looked at his own police uniform hanging in the closet. He only worked part-time now but every time he put his uniform on he thought of him. And when he looked at Anna who, although her eyes were brown and Alex's were blue, they both had that same saucer-like shape that people had commented on since they were born. He remembered him whenever he saw a squad car, a cop, whether on the street or patrolling fictitious roads on TV. And whenever he thought of Alex, he remembered his darling Teresa—his first and only grandchild that held a special place in his heart since the day he held her in his arms just a few hours after her birth. Helena never got over the fact that he held her first. Teresa loved all her grandparents but there was no question from those that saw the two of them together that Teresa had a special affection for her Opa John.

"Opa, let's play," she would say when she saw him walk in the door on the several times a week he would visit. He would scoop her up in his huge arms and squat down on the floor with her to play dolls, Legos, or whatever she wanted to do. The officers John commanded would never believe this was the authoritative chief of police who once gave them orders, the man who calmly and quickly took charge in the worst of situations. The man who never winced at a dead body (except when he made the coroner show him Alex's and Teresa's.) Those cops would never believe he would sit and sip tea with dolls at a make-believe tea party. That he would pick up a tiny pink teacup in his rough hands with the daintiness of a princess.

"You know they're always on my mind. But so is Gina. Although you've erased every trace of her in this house and won't allow any of us to stay in contact with her, she's still in our hearts—in mine, anyway."

"I just can't believe you would still want to see her after what she did."

John rolled his eyes. "Oh, don't start with that 'this is all her fault' nonsense."

He couldn't bear to hear Helena go on another time about how Gina never should have had her friend Elizabeth watch Teresa that day so Gina could run some errands, which included planning a special dinner for her and Alex.

"Well, if she wasn't so concerned about seducing her husband, she wouldn't have had to take Teresa to Elizabeth's."

"It's called a marriage! You know spending quality time with your spouse. But no, I guess you can't understand that."

She ignored this comment, like she overlooked the distance she kept from him since Alex died, from everyone for that matter, and kept pressing the issue.

"Why couldn't *I* have watched her? We are only a few minutes away and then this never would have happened."

John walked away instead of getting into this argument which had been played out dozens of times.

"I wish she did leave Teresa here but Gina was in that accident," she almost shrieked. "All our lives would have been better."

John turned around quickly.

"Is that what you've been dying to say all these months? You really wish Alex were alive to grieve his beloved wife?"

"We all would have been better off. I wish she never came into our lives."

"Gina is part of this family. You always thought of

her as a daughter and now you talk about her in ways that disgusts and embarrasses me. I don't know why I allowed you to keep all of us from her for this long."

He slammed the door behind him but not before she whipped it open once more.

"John Andros, if you go over there don't even think about walking back into this house. Do you hear me?"

Chapter 9

The creak made Gina bolt upright from where she lie on the couch looking at Lester Holt on the television but not hearing a word he was saying. Whether it was the wind or just the settling of the house it always unnerved her for at least an hour after its wake. She heard the sound again. Were her parents back? Did they feel bad for storming off? She pulled the curtain in the front room ever so slightly, but saw no car. She noticed the trees were still which just increased her panic level. If it wasn't the wind, what was it? She heard the soft thump again. Gina walked down the hallway to her bedroom. Though it only took a few seconds it felt like several minutes until she reached her bedside table where she kept the gun now. She opened the oak drawer and pulled out her familiar friend—the only thing that could give her some semblance of calmness—if you could call it that. She ran her thumb against the Glock and placed the gun firmly in her hand. She put her finger on the trigger and quickly walked back down the hallway with soft steps so no one would hear her. When she reached the front room again, she heard the source of her anxiety—a dog barking. The stupid thing must have been rustling in the bushes earlier. She sat down on the couch but her hand never moved from its position on the gun.

Thirty minutes must have passed, and Gina's stomach slowly started to unwind from the tightly wrapped wad of nerves that were wound up like a huge ball of rubber bands. She still sat in the same position, but now the gun seemed like an evil adversary who was willing her to do something that would end her pain. Usually after she was frightened, she would eventually put the gun away but today she couldn't do it. It seemed to be speaking to her.

"I will end your misery. You won't have to think of them every second. You won't endure this anguish any longer. You won't have to worry about your mother-in-law who has turned the whole family against you. You won't have to live with this gaping hole where your heart once lived."

She raised her arm only for a second then lowered it again and spoke aloud: "I rebuke you Satan in the name of Jesus. I won't give you this power over me."

Then Gina heard a knock on the door. Without thinking she walked over and opened it with her left hand. John's face turned a sick shade of milk when he looked down and saw what was firmly placed in Gina's right fist.

"Gina, give me the gun."

"Gina," he said again, this time with more force.

He stepped forward to gently take it out of her hand.

Suddenly Gina awakened from her immobile state, jerked her hand away so John couldn't take the gun, but he was too strong for the frailness that had become her body.

"Gina, I want to help you."

"Please give me back the gun."

"It was a mistake for me to leave this with you."

"No, it wasn't. I just heard something, and I was checking it out but it turned out to be a dog."

"Gina, I'm taking this with me. But, come on, sit down, let's talk."

"No! Just give me the gun back."

"I'll be by later to talk to you once you have calmed down. I'm here for you Gina. I don't know why I've stayed away but that's changing now."

"Gee, thanks. Where the hell have you been?" Gina then stopped as these words were so unlike her but they actually were making her feel better, were giving her some of her feistiness back.

"I'm sorry, Gina."

"Don't be sorry. Just give me back the gun and go back to your wife."

"Goodbye, Gina."

She grabbed him as he was walking out the door.

"John, please! I swear I won't hurt myself but please let me have it. It makes me calm. You know how scared I get."

As she was begging, John pulled her toward him but she resisted. He kept trying to envelop her in his arms and finally she was too tired to fight. She let him hug her but wouldn't let herself melt in the comfort of his arms. After being like that for a while Gina turned away hoping John would realize that this was all she could take right now.

"I'll be back, Gina. I'm here for you now."

She stood there and watched him go hoping he would stand by his words, but the accident had taught her she couldn't count on anyone.

Chapter 10

The fierce knocking on the door made Anna drop the Pottery Barn catalog she was looking at in her pile of mail. She knew it could only be one person waiting for her to answer.

"Hello, mother," she said as she opened the door.

"Do you know where your father is right now?" Helena asked.

Although her mother was acting like her father had just run off with a neighbor to have a torrid affair, Anna knew this was just another one of those situations in which her mother was making a simple situation dramatic. He probably forgot to fold his clothes properly or some other trivial matter that grated on her nerves.

"Mom, calm down, I'm sure he's just out for a walk or he ran to the--."

"He's at Gina's."

Anna stopped admiring the periwinkle sheets from

Pottery Barn and dropped the catalog on the counter.

"What happened?"

"I don't want to get into it but after Maria and Sal left ..."

"Wait. Back up. Maria and Sal were here?"

"Listen, Anna, I don't have time to explain every minute detail to you."

"I don't think the fact that we're finally mentioning Gina's name is a minute detail. You forbid us to see her, to comfort her after the accident. So, essentially you made us lose three family members that day."

"She's not family!"

"She's not?" Anna walked briskly to her mahogany bookshelf and pulled down her photo album. She flipped through the pages and immediately found the one she was searching for. After all, she knew it by heart.

"Look at this photo of you and Gina at Christmas two years ago. Remember? That was the year she bought you that bracelet you loved so much. My God, you wore it every day until after the accident when you decided you hated her, so you threw it in the garbage."

"I don't have time for this."

Anna flipped a few more pages until she found the other memory she was searching for.

"Look at this one of you in the delivery room with them when Teresa was born. I hate to break it to you Mom but these aren't pictures of casual acquaintances. These are the photos of people who shared in each other's lives--who cared about each other."

Anna then wasn't as concerned with her mother. She again became absorbed in the photos as if she hadn't seen them in years. Her hand rested on her favorite—of Anna and Gina at Gina's 30th birthday party last year. Anna and Alex had planned it expertly and Gina didn't suspect a thing. She was so surprised and touched by everything Anna had done for the party from the elaborate decorations to the delicious Italian food. After all, it was a big deal that Anna deviated from her Greek roots to make Gina's favorite dishes including bruschetta, lasagna and cannoli. Though Helena had griped at first, she even complimented Anna on what a great job she had done.

Anna looked up and saw Helena glancing at the pictures though she quickly turned away when Anna caught her eye.

"Do you think I walked over here to walk down memory lane?"

"Why did you come here, Mom?"

"Forget it, this was a mistake. I should have known you would take his side."

"What? I didn't even say anything. In fact, I haven't said a word to you about this since you banished her from our lives."

"You want to be best friends with her. Fine, be my guest. Go over there and chat it up for hours for all I care. Why don't you and your father move in there."

Anna just ignored her mother's theatrics.

"Look Mom, I'm embarrassed to admit this but I was so distraught over losing my brother that I bought into your demented story that Gina was responsible for his death."

"She is responsible."

"Mom, let me finish."

"Once some time passed, I finally admitted that wasn't true but I stayed away because I knew how mad you would be if I went over there."

"Stop it Anna, you're a grown woman. You can do what you want."

"You mean if I had gone over there, or Christian, you wouldn't have stopped talking to us?"

"You wouldn't have held a grudge against me like you did against your sister when she kept spending time with Lydia. Just because Lydia and you didn't get along you thought your sister shouldn't talk to her either. Anyway, the only reason I went along with this and never said anything is because I knew how much you were hurting. How much you still are. I know you loved them more than anything. Look, I can't even say their names around you. We all had to tiptoe around you because …"

"What do you mean, we?" Helena yelled though she didn't wait for an answer. "So you, your father and Christian talked about me behind my back."

"Mom, calm down like we said we were worried about you. Not talking about all of this was your way with dealing with the pain but we couldn't do that. We needed to remember them."

"So, you discussed how horrible I was for not sitting and looking at photo albums all day and crying. For not going over to have tea with Gina. You mean I should have sat there with her while all the time I thought that if it weren't for her my son and my beautiful granddaughter would still be alive."

"Look, Mom, obviously we still disagree. But I've tiptoed around this for too long. Gina is our family. She was like a sister to me and I'm glad Dad is over there."

Helena slammed the album shut then left.

~

Anna knocked on Gina's door three times but there was no answer, so she opened it slightly.

"Is anyone here?"

Silence was the only answer.

She stood in the living room and saw photos of Alex, Teresa and Gina everywhere. The musty smell of wine was faint but it stood out since it was so different than the strawberry and citrus aromas that usually floated through the rooms. Gina was always known for her love of scented candles and had them burning constantly. Even after Teresa started toddling around, Gina simply moved them to places where her little hands couldn't wreak havoc. Anna walked over to look closer at some of the photos. She couldn't see them clearly from where she stood earlier, though she was only a few feet away. There were no lights on yet Gina's Camry sat in the driveway.

Teresa's portraits at three-, six-, nine-months and one year were all hanging in an arc on the main wall over the entertainment center. No one else would have noticed it but Anna couldn't help think that Teresa's 2-year photo should have hung there. The accident happened shortly before her second birthday. Then there were the prints of Alex and Gina at their wedding and the one of the entire Andros clan at Teresa's baptism. More than 50 people celebrated at her mother's house.

No longer wanting to look at the reminders strewn all over the room she walked down the narrow hallway. She was about to call out for Gina again but lost her voice at what she saw. Gina was pulling a shirt over her head and while her breasts were covered her belly was exposed. Seeing the bulge in Gina's normally toned tummy caused Anna to drop the keys she had been holding in her hands.

Gina swung around and saw her sister-in-law standing there. Anna stood silently staring. Though she tried with all her strength to open her mouth it seemed glued shut. Gina's dark Italian mane that was always silky smooth looked as if it hadn't been washed or even brushed in a week. Her face that once was the picture of perfection now included dark crevices under her eyes and wrinkles near her cheeks where a smile once lived. Instead of the beautiful 30-year-old Anna remembered, Gina now looked much older.

"My God, I'm going be an aunt again," Anna finally uttered when her larynx was finally freed.

And as her father had done merely an hour earlier, Anna embraced this person who she once thought of as her own sister. Anna felt Gina lean in and place her hand on Anna's back. Gina was more reserved than she had ever been with her sister-in-law but Anna sensed that for the first time since the accident Gina was finally sharing her grief with someone.

"I can't believe it," said Anna. "What did Dad say? Oh my God I can't wait to plan your shower."

"Anna," Gina said with a finality that brought that discussion to a close before it even started.

"Okay, forget that for now," said Anna, acknowledging the extreme absurdity of that statement. That would have been fine a year ago but the two haven't spoken in months and here Anna was acting like things were normal.

"I didn't tell him," said Gina, bringing Anna back to the unfamiliar present though she wanted to stay in the past—before the accident.

"What?"

"I haven't heard from anyone in your family for months, who by the way I used to talk to every day. Now all of a sudden both you and John drop by on the same day and I'm supposed to go back to the way things were."

"It seems so weird to hear you call him John."

"Spare me, Anna. You want me to call him dear old Dad? To hug him and tell him all about the baby."

"Let's talk about the baby. Is it a boy or a girl? When's your due date? How have your appointments been going?"

"I don't want to talk about it."

"Are you still going to Dr. Bellini? I know how much you loved her. What did your parents say, they must be so excited?"

"They don't know."

"What?"

"You heard me," said Gina as sat on the bed in her room. The last thing she needed was for Anna to want to go in the kitchen to chat and see the cabernet bottle on the table and the empty one in the garbage.

"Who knows?"

"You."

"That's it? Well, at least you can talk to your doctor. What does she say? I know she must be watching you extra carefully given your fragile situation. Is everything okay with the baby?" She stopped again, knowing she was going too far. But when talking to Gina it was so easy to go that familiar place.

"I guess. Listen, Anna, I really don't want to talk about it and you better swear you won't tell anyone."

"I won't, but they're going to find out sooner or later. I'm actually surprised you've hid it this long. You must be five months along by now right?

"Something like that."

"Well, you're not going to be able to hide it forever. I can't believe your parents didn't notice, though you are pretty small. Are you taking care of yourself?"

"Why are you here?"

"I finally realized how stupid I was being and want to make it right. And this is an even bigger reason to reconcile."

"I appreciate this, Anna, but I'm really tired so I need to get some sleep."

Anna hugged her and told her she'd be back. She turned to close the door and saw Gina standing near the photos rubbing her bulging stomach.

~

When Anna was just a few paces from her doorstep she wondered if she had passed anyone in the few blocks that she walked from Gina's house. The millions of thoughts that were vying for attention overwhelmed her and put her in a daze. A few minutes later she almost tripped on her father, who was sitting on her front stoop, talking on the phone. He hung up right before she sat down next to him.

"Anna, what's wrong?"

"I could ask you the same thing."

Her father seemed to have aged since she saw him yesterday. It may have been her imagination but she noticed more lines in his face and more gray in his already almost all silver locks.

"Well, if I look worried it's because I went to see Gina."

"I know, I just came from there."

"You did? How was she? Was she better?"

"What do you mean? Dad, tell me what's going on."

John told her everything, and Anna couldn't believe this was the same woman she knew before the accident.

"Dad, I feel awful. I was so wrapped up in my own grief that I didn't think of what this was doing to her."

"I didn't either. And I should know better. Can you imagine the pain Gina wakes up with every day in that house? The constant reminders she is bombarded with. I'm finally allowing myself to think of the agony she's going through but I don't know what to do. But we can't just let her be there all alone while drowning her sorrows in alcohol. And I saw the cabinets when I was there. There is no food in them. I don't think she eats much of anything."

Anna's hands began shaking again as they did when she first saw Gina earlier but this time she caught her keys before they fell to the ground.

"What do you mean drowning her sorrows?"

"Didn't you notice the wine bottles?"

"No, I was too excited about …"

"About what?"

Anna sat silently and all the pieces finally started to fit together. The non-answers to her questions about the baby. The fact that Gina was hardly showing. The wine bottles. The lack of food. The darkness in the house that echoed Gina's constant state of mind. The fact that she has told no one about the baby. Gina was in complete denial.

"I was just excited to see her again," she said eager to change the subject. "Who were you just on the phone with?"

"Gina's Dad."

"I thought you just saw her parents today?"

"I did, but after I saw her with a gun, I had to let them know. I may not be the one who can help her right now but I need to make sure she is getting the right help for her mental health."

"So, how did that conversation go?"

"Well, they were already freaking out about the whole situation, so take a guess. But in the end, they thanked me for calling. They hung up with me to call the leader of that grief group she is supposed to be going to."

"Supposed to?"

"Apparently, she hasn't been showing up."

"Dad, do you know how bad we screwed up here?"

"I know, Anna."

"No, I don't think you do. She is all alone, well, besides Elizabeth. I am sure she has stuck by her thank goodness. But she isn't a licensed therapist. And she doesn't know about the baby either. I guess Gina has been avoiding her too, and she is barely showing anyway. She needs someone to help her work through her grief."

"I know, Anna, but I don't think it's our place anymore. Her parents are taking care of her."

"Really, is that why they just left her in a dark house with no power, and walking around with a gun?"

"That's why I called them Anna. We need to let them handle it. I know you love her, but they have a point. They can't keep enabling her. She has to want to move forward."

None of that helped put Anna's fears to rest. Her

Dad didn't know the half of it, and now wasn't the right time to tell him. She had her own call to the Galliano's to make.

~

"Hello," came the familiar voice through the phone.

"Mr. Galliano, this is Anna Andros."

"Is something wrong with Gina?"

"I think you need to come here right away. I have something to tell you, and I want to do it in person."

"I told Gina I'm not going to baby her anymore. I've tried and tried to get her to face reality and she won't. It's up to her now."

"My Dad told me you were going to try to get her to go back to that grief group. Is she going now?"

"I can't make her do that either, Anna. But I called the leader and asked her to reach out to her. When she figures out it's time to move on, I'll be there but I won't watch her destroy herself."

"Mr. Galliano—stop! It's not just about her anymore. There's a baby."

Anna heard a gasp followed by the phone crashing on the floor and knew it was Mrs. Galliano who must have been listening in on another line.

"We'll be at your apartment in about two hours."

"No, meet me at The Creamery instead."

"Why? Oh, of course, God forbid your mother should find us at your apartment. Heaven knows the wrath you would endure for that one. Fine, I don't want to risk seeing her anyway because God knows what I would do to her after the way she has treated my daughter."

"Mr. Galliano, she's grieving too."

"Save it, Anna. Oh, and when we get there don't

bring up your mother."

Anna opened her mouth but decided against it. She was done worrying about her mother. It was time to concentrate on Gina—the person who really needed help.

~

Maria Galliano had cried every day since the accident over Gina, Alex, Teresa--over all the horrible details of those losses and what they did to her daughter. Some days there were less tears than others but every day her daughter was in pain so was Maria. But all that paled in comparison to the flood being cast out of her eyes.

Even though she couldn't see him because her vision was dangerously blurred, she knew Sal must be looking at her with a mixture of sadness and concern. He worried about Gina in his own way but Maria knew Sal thought she was overly consumed by Gina's grief. Imagine what he thought of her now as she sat here with liquid seeping steadily out of her eyes. They left Anna 15 minutes ago and the tears had not subsided. Sal hadn't even tried to talk to her as it was no use attempting to be heard over her sobs.

"Maria, please try to get a hold of yourself."

She was a little surprised by the amount of caring she heard in his tone. Sal was always uncomfortable with tears and this was by far the most hysterical she had ever been.

She took a deep breath, wiped her drenched face with several tissues and attempted some words.

"I don't know where to start, Sal. There's just so much."

"I know."

For the first time in his life Maria sensed that Sal didn't know how to fix the situation. Maria decided she would try to take control, as ludicrous as that sounded in the state she was in.

"When Anna called us she told us about the baby. That was a huge bit of news right there. But then we get there, and Anna tells us not just of a baby, but of her drinking every night."

"Maria."

"Wait, I need to talk about this. This is what happened when we left her alone Sal."

"I'm sorry. I know now how much she needs help. The more we leave her alone, the more out of control she gets. She can push us away if she wants but we have to keep pushing."

"This is all *her* fault."

"Come on Maria, let's not focus on Helena. We need to concentrate our energy on how to help our daughter."

"Sal, if she hadn't ostracized her from that family she loved so much, maybe she wouldn't have gotten this bad."

"We already tried going over to the Andros'. Remember how that turned out? We need to forget about them. She's our daughter and we need to help her. And we just need to keep praying for her."

"But we tried. Remember when we made her go to that grief group? She didn't last more than a few sessions. All she talked about was how they couldn't understand how it felt to lose a husband and a child."

"That was only a month after the deaths. Maybe it was too soon. I didn't realize it then but I do now. She really needs help—to go back to that group--and we need to be there for her every step of the way. We need to remind her she can rely on God to help her through this."

Maria reached for her husband's hand. Maybe they would be able to help Gina this time. Maybe this child would give them all something to look forward to.

Chapter 11

Gina glanced at her phone and was shocked to see she had almost ten texts. When she looked she found most of them were from Anna. What was she going to do now that Anna knew about the baby? Now that someone other than her knew she was pregnant it seemed real. But that didn't mean she was ready to address it. And she certainly wasn't going to turn to Anna for help.

"Lord, what do I do?"

"Lean on Me."

She looked at her Bible on the bedside table where it always lived, though she hadn't opened its pages since before the accident and still wasn't ready to do so now. But she knew she needed help.

"I can do all things through Christ who strengthens me."

It was the verse her father had taught her since she was a little girl and always came to her when she was hurting.

She picked up her cell phone and dialed.

"Mom, I need help."

~

Sal looked at his wife who hardly spoke since they started the drive two hours ago.

"What are you going to say to her, Maria?"

"She called us, Sal. It must mean she is ready to tell us about the baby. First, I'm just going to listen and be there for her."

He reached over and took her hand. "You are an amazing mother you know that?"

~

Maria knocked on the door and Gina opened it immediately and embraced her mother in a strong hug. She looked over at her father who was peeking past the doorway and saw the huge relief on his face that the lights were on.

"Hi, Dad."

"Hey, where is my hug?"

"Right here," she said, and then enfolded him as well. They walked in the house and took in the very different sight from the last time they were here. There were no bills piled on the kitchen table. There was some food on the counter and Maria noticed that Gina looked the best she had since the accident.

"Mom. Dad. Sit down I need to talk to you. First, I want to thank you for everything you have done for me. As you can see, I am getting a little better. At least I am able to do some basic tasks to take care of myself."

"We are proud of you, Gina."

"Thanks, Dad. You know Philippians 4:13 is what helped me get through these past few months and get a little stronger. Thank you."

Sal sat silent and Maria could see the glistening in his eyes.

"Listen I need to tell you both something. I'm pregnant."

"Anna told us," said Maria.

"I guess I am not surprised. Thanks for giving me a few days to reach out to you on my own."

"What changed, Gina?"

"I know you guys think I am crazy but really until Anna found out it honestly didn't seem real. I mean no one knew. I just couldn't deal with it. Then when she saw me that day everything seemed to change."

"Have you been to the doctor?" her Dad asked.

"I have. The baby is smaller than she would have liked. But I was honest and told her everything. She is watching me closely. I am finally taking care of myself."

"Gina. We are so proud of you."

"Thanks, Dad. I know what I did was wrong but I can't beat myself up over it. I am really trying to rely on God and move forward from this point."

"That's amazing, Gina," said her Mom. "But promise me you will lean on others also. Can you please go see a therapist? Or at least go back to that grief group. This isn't going to be easy to go through this. It's going to bring back a lot of memories."

"Believe me I know, and yes I will get some help. And fair warning, I plan on leaning on you two a lot."

"I'm so proud of you, Gina. Have you talked to Anna since that day?"

"She calls and texts me all the time but I don't want to talk to her. But I did text her the other day to tell her I saw a doctor and that everything is okay and that she needs to leave me alone."

"Do you know if she told the family?"

"I have no idea."

~

The Andros family was gathered for its weekly Sunday dinner. When the plates had been cleared, Anna told her parents and Christian they needed to talk.

"There is no way to say this, so I am just going to blurt it out. Gina is pregnant."

"Is it …"

"Yes Mom, it's Alex's."

"But that would make her …"

"About 6 months pregnant, yes."

Anna told her how she found out, and that Gina said the baby is okay but wants nothing to do with Anna.

"Can you blame her?" said Christian who had been silent until now.

"No, I guess I can't."

"Dad, have you been to see her since that day …"

John immediately felt guilty. He vowed when he saw her with the gun, he would check on her but he never did. The wrath he would have faced from Helena made him stay away.

"I'm going over there," said Helena. "John, go get in the car."

~

They were making the short ten-minute drive to Gina's and John kept telling Helena what a bad idea this was.

"You haven't talked to her all this time. You can't just march in there because she is pregnant."

"That is my grandchild, John. Watch me."

They pulled up to the house and John tried to take

some semblance of control though his wife took that away from him long ago.

"Helena. I'm going first," and he barged ahead of her holding her back.

"John. What are you doing here?" Gina said with disdain as she opened the door and saw Helena standing behind him.

"I really don't want to see either of you."

"We know you are pregnant, Gina," said Helena as she marched past John and surveyed the state of the house. She seemed displeased that it was actually clean and in order.

"This is my grandchild, and I will be here."

"So, you haven't spoken to me for all these months and now you expect things to change? That's not happening Helena. I told Anna I am fine. The baby is healthy. I am taking care of us. That's all you need to know. I really need both of you to leave. I am expecting company," then she ushered them out the door.

~

"I'm so proud of you, Gina," said Elizabeth as they sat on Gina's couch surrounded by the amazing food her friend had brought her.

"Thanks. I'm really trying. I used to sit here after the accident praying they would come over to see me but no one ever did. So now I am just filled with hurt and anger."

"I know but you have to try to let some of that go. It can't be good for you or the baby."

"You are right but I don't want to see them. I feel more hopeful than I ever have. There is a part of Alex inside me. It's sad but I feel it's a new beginning and I want to be strong for the baby. I want to get better and move forward and I have to leave them behind."

"I get it. But you know this isn't going to be easy right? That family is quite determined."

"Don't remind me--let's talk about other things. I found out the sex of the baby."

"Why are you just now telling me this? Oh my gosh spill it."

"It's a boy," then she smiled, and a single tear ran down her cheek. "I'm going to name him Alex."

"Oh, Gina. You know this is a blessing from God, right?"

"I do. And I will continue to thank him for it every day."

~

Helena and John walked back in the house with Helena still spewing awful things about Gina.

"I'm done, Helena. You need to stop. She has every right to cut us out after what we did to her. We just need to give her time and treat her with respect and kindness. You really think there is any hope with you treating her that way? You think she is going to run to you for baby advice? Sometimes I just wonder where your brain is. I'm going upstairs. Hopefully you can be calmer about this tomorrow."

~

Helena called Anna, and her daughter barely said hello before she started in.

"Do you believe she is going to keep us from that baby? I won't let that happen."

"Mom, stop. Please tell me you didn't go over there shouting demands at her. Were you at least a little civil?"

The silence was her answer.

"If you won't help me, Christian will," then she hung up.

~

"Mom. I'm not helping you. I have guilt over this every day. I was so close with Gina—she was my sister. I can't be like you and try to talk to her now and expect her to forget the way we treated her. We have to give her time."

"Now you sound like your sister."

"Well, Anna is very smart."

"Fine, I will handle this without you," and for the second time that day she hung up on another one of her children vowing to handle this alone.

~

"John, I need you to drop me off at an appointment today."

"What time?"

"11:00. I will just call you when I am done, and you can pick me up."

"Where am I taking you, Helena?" They were in the car and Helena kept telling him they were almost there. Where he didn't know.

"There it is. Pull over."

Helena got out of the car and he looked at the sign: Attorney at Law.

"What was she up to?" John wondered.

"John, what are you doing in here?" asked Helena as she sat in the lobby waiting for her appointment.

"What are you doing here, Helena? Are you crazy? This is about the baby isn't it?"

"She is not fit to raise a child. I have proof of that. The alcohol. The unpaid bills that went on for months."

"She was grieving. None of that is happening now.

She is finally getting her life together and it's because of the baby."

"He will see you now," interrupted the woman at the front desk.

"We won't be staying," said John, as he grabbed his wife by the arm and forced her out of there.

"John Andros. You have no right!"

"Helena, stop! I have every right. I have let you do crazy things before but not this time. I am taking control and you are not causing problems for Gina anymore."

Helena stayed silent the entire ride home but John knew she was plotting her next move.

~

John Andros had never been much of a prayer. But he didn't know what else to do. Gina was the one who had brought religion into their lives when she and Alex started dating. Still, he never really talked to God much until Alex and Teresa landed in the hospital.

"Dear, Lord, I don't know what else to do. I am sorry I didn't stop this before it got this far. Please let Helena realize this is wrong. She needs to leave Gina alone. Please work in this family to somehow bring us all together. Amen."

John then picked up his phone and sent a group text to Christian and Anna. "Who can meet for lunch today?"

~

The three Andros' family members sat at their favorite Greek café while Christian and Anna waited for their Dad to tell them the latest thing their mother had done.

"She went to see a lawyer today. But I stopped her

before she met with him."

"What? Is she crazy?"

"Calm down, Anna," said Christian.

"I will not. This time she has gone too far. It was about the baby right? She was going to try to get custody?"

"That's what I'm thinking," said John.

"Dad, what are we going to do?" asked Christian.

"I honestly don't know. But I've started praying."

The two siblings exchanged glances.

"I know. It surprised me too."

Anna reached her hand across the table to grab her father's. "It's okay, Dad. We will figure it out. Maybe you have the right idea. Maybe God is the only one who can help us now."

~

Anna and Christian watched their father drive away and Christian started in before Anna could say anything.

"Listen, Anna. I know what you're going to say and you can't do it."

"What am I going to do?"

"You want to march over there to Mom's and ream her out for this. But you know she won't listen. It's Mom. She is going to do what she wants."

"So we are going to stand by as she tries to take Gina's baby away? The baby is the only reason Gina is even getting better now."

"I agree. But going to reason with Mom won't do any good."

"Wow, maybe Dad has the right idea after all. Maybe we should just get down on our knees because that really may be the only thing that can stop her."

"I think we should warn Gina," said Christian. "She has to be prepared for our mother."

~

When Christian pulled up to Gina's house, he noticed the overgrown lawn, the trees that were way past needing to be trimmed, and all the other areas of the yard that had been neglected since Alex died.

"Christian, what's wrong? Why aren't you getting out of the car?"

"I just can't believe I abandoned her," he said while wiping a stray tear from the corner of his eye. "Look at this place. It's a mess. I didn't come over and help her with all this. I mean someone must have been mowing the lawn for her. But who? It should have been me. He was my brother, and I loved her too. He would be so angry with me on how I handled all this. And all I can think about now is the hurt I saw in her eyes when I ignored her at the funeral. She didn't deserve that from me."

"We screwed up, Christian. But all we can do is move on and try to help her."

"Why are we doing this now, Anna? Because of the baby? That's what she is going to think. We may be too late."

~

"What are you guys doing here?" asked Gina as she opened the door dressed in an oversized top, no doubt to hide her growing belly even though it still looked like a small bump in her shapely figure. "Didn't you get the hint when I ignored your texts? I don't want to see you. I am finally moving forward. Why can't you just let me?"

"We aren't the ones trying to stop you, Gina," said

Anna.

She looked from one sibling to the other.

"What has your mother done now?"

"She tried to meet with a lawyer," answered Christian.

"What?"

"Calm down. Dad stopped her."

"Christian, we all know no one can stop Helena. Why is she doing this?" as she wiped her eye with the corner of her sleeve.

"That's why we are here. You need to know what she has planned. You may want to get a lawyer of your own."

The tears were streaming heavily now, and her body was starting to shake.

"I can't deal with this, do you understand me? I am trying to move forward--for myself and the baby. I can't do this."

Anna took her hand. "You can, Gina, and you don't have to do it alone. We are so sorry we weren't here before. We can't take that back but we are here now--for good."

"Anna is right. Words can't take back how we treated you but we just hope you can forgive us and let us be here for you from now on."

Gina lay her head on Christian's shoulder and let the tears flow. The two siblings just held her while she grieved in silence for several minutes before uttering, "Do you want some good news? It's a boy," then she continued to cry.

~

"Christian, what's wrong?" his sister asked as they walked to the car.

"I just keep thinking of Alex. How happy he would be to be having a boy. I keep thinking of her all alone and all the extra grief Mom is causing her. I just hope she can get through this."

~

Gina stood outside the door. She knew everyone was already in there. Maybe she should have gotten here earlier so she didn't have to walk in and have them all stare. But if she got here before the meeting, she would have had to make small talk with people.

You can do this, Gina. I can do all things through Christ who strengthens me. Then she walked in the door and took the only open seat she saw—the one next to pasty hand.

As soon as she entered the room all eyes moved to her belly though they tried to pretend they didn't notice her swelling stomach.

"Gina, it's nice to see you again," said Dr. Roberts.

"I'm happy to be here. Thank you all for welcoming me back."

~

When the meeting was over, Gina turned to pasty hand. "I'm sorry I don't remember your name."

"I'm Grace. It's so nice to see you here. Will you be back next week?"

"I will."

"Well, I look forward to seeing you. You hang in there," she said before walking away.

Grace. Maybe Grace was meant to find her.

~

Gina sat at her laptop, her hair piled up on a messy bun on top of her head, a style Alex always loved, looked at the Google search box and typed, "lawyers near me." She knew Helena too well to even consider she would leave this alone. Gina had to be ready.

David Swanson was a distinguished looking man in his forties. While dressed in a black power suit, somehow Gina didn't find him intimidating as she had feared. In fact, she felt comfortable spilling the story about her mother-in-law, her grief, the drinking earlier in the pregnancy, and that she was worried Helena would try to take the baby.

"Alright let's start building our case."

"What do you mean?"

"I need everything there is to know about Helena Andros."

"Like dirt? I don't want to drag her through the mud. I just want to move forward with my baby and try to get past this overwhelming grief. I'm really trying and making progress."

"I believe you are. But that's not how this works. Does she have a good reputation in the community?"

"Yes."

"Will she have people speak to that when they are called as character witnesses?"

"Yes."

"Do others know you were drinking?"

"Stop. I get it."

"I'm not sure you do. I'm not saying you won't prevail but we have to be ready."

"But I'm not. I don't have this fight in me. I am just getting some strength to take care of myself and the baby. I don't have the energy for this."

"Well, you better dig deep because like it or not you are going to have to face this and fight."

~

Gina was barely in her front door, when she went right to the cabinet, took a wine glass and reached for a bottle from the wine rack, forgetting there was none in the house. She dropped on her knees right there on the hard tile floor and prayed.

"Dear, God. Please turn Helena's heart. Please don't have her go after the baby. I will even forgive her if she asks me. I will let her into the baby's life. Just don't have her hate me and fight me for my child. Please, Lord give me strength to get through this. I can't do it alone."

For her next meeting with the lawyer Gina was ready. She shored up her nerves and if she had to fight, she knew she could do it. He noticed the difference as soon as she walked in his office in her black slacks and fitted white blouse, all showing off her trim figure, despite her small baby bump.

"Please have a seat. Let me show you what I prepared." Gina said a silent prayer, then sat down next to him at the small conference table as he explained their next moves.

"If she is going to take action, Gina, she will have someone serve you papers. It's been three weeks since you found out she tried to see that lawyer. I am sure she rescheduled another appointment. So if she is going to do this, I expect it will be soon."

"Wait, before you go on, tell me about the lawyer she hired. What do you know about him?"

The way his dark brow furrowed above his salty blue eyes, said it all. This wasn't going to be easy.

"He's tough. But don't worry about that. I'm tougher."

He picked up his gold-plated pen, and legal

notebook, and said, "You have to tell me everything you have done that she may hold against you."

Gina finished her stories. The wine. The break down in Publix. The not really admitting there was a baby for months. Then she waited for him to tell her how bad it was.

"Gina. Your husband and daughter died. It's almost a miracle you are sitting in my office right now looking as good as you do. Is it great? No. But it's not enough for her to take custody. I'll start preparing our response now, so we are ready if she tries to make a case."

~

Helena looked down at her Coach watch with gold band and shifted nervously on the couch in the ornate front sitting room in her house. She knew she would be getting word any minute that it had been done. She just wanted to know.

~

When Gina opened the door the tall scrawny man said her name, "Gina Andros." When she nodded, he served her the papers.

"Wait. I have something for you too."

She had them right on the table by the door for when this moment came.

"Here you can take this back to your firm. It's my response to Mrs. Andros' complaint."

~

It was seven now and Helena should have heard back from her lawyer at least an hour ago. Just as she was about to call him and demand an answer the phone started ringing.

"Was she shocked?" she asked abruptly.

"Not exactly. We need to talk."

"I'm listening."

"She knew this was coming. She hired her own lawyer—a good one in fact—and had her own response ready. Can you come to my office tomorrow and I can go over it with you?"

"Yes, I will be there," then hung up knowing exactly who it was that warned Gina. The only other person who knew was John.

~

Christian rolled his eyes when he saw the name on the caller ID but knew he had to pick up.

"Hi, Mom."

"Christian, I need you to drive me somewhere in the morning."

"Sure. What time and where to?"

"Not far. I'll tell you when you get here," and she hung up.

~

"Hey, Mom you look even fancier than normal," as he saw her in her perfectly pressed pants and tailored blouse. "Where are you going?"

"I have an appointment. It's on Prince Street."

When they turned the corner on Prince, she stopped him. You can just drop me off here. I want to take a little walk.

"Are you sure?"

"Absolutely honey. Thanks for the ride."

"Do you need me to come get you?"

"No that's okay I will find a ride home. Maybe I will call your sister."

"Okay, see you later."

Once he circled the block a few times he figured she would be at her appointment by now.

He knew his mother well enough to know she was up to something. So, he drove down one block to Prince Street and immediately saw the law offices on the right.

~

"Anna."

"Christian, what's wrong?"

"Mom's at the lawyer's office again."

"Wait, how do you know?"

"Because I dropped her there?"

"What?"

"Well I didn't know that's where she was going but now I am pretty sure that's where she is. This is bad, Anna. You need to talk to her."

"Why me?"

"You are the only one she will listen to."

She knew he was right but this would be tough even for her. Helena Andros didn't change her mind for anyone.

~

Helena could not believe what she was hearing. This supposedly amazing lawyer was telling her he didn't think she had much of a case based on Gina's response. How did Gina get a better lawyer than she did?

"What do you mean I have to give up?"

"Mrs. Andros. It's all there. Look it over. We can fight this but it will be a long drawn out battle that we don't have an overwhelming chance of winning. Wouldn't it just be easier if you tried to make amends so you can be part of her life and the baby's?"

"If you're not up to this job I will find someone who is." She grabbed the response out of his hands and walked out the door. She wasn't in the mood to talk to anyone but did need a ride home so dialed Anna who picked up right away.

"Anna, honey. I'm downtown today. Christian dropped me off earlier for an appointment. Do you want to meet me for lunch then you can drive me home?"

"Sure, Mom. See you in about 15 minutes."

~

They had just ordered their food and Anna knew she couldn't wait any longer.

"Mom, I know where you were today. I know you are hurting. But why are you doing this? You know Alex wouldn't want this. He would be so angry with you right now."

The blood drained from her mother's face.

"Let's go, Anna."

"Fine I will take you home."

"No, we are stopping at the station."

"What, are you crazy?"

"You are taking me there, Anna."

"Dad is going to be furious. He doesn't have time for your nonsense when he is working."

"Drive."

~

"Helena, what a pleasant surprise, said the officer on duty at the station desk. "Is John expecting you?"

"He isn't. I want to surprise him."

"Of course, I will call him."

John walked in, and for a second was happy to see his wife and daughter. It had been a long time since they stopped by. Usually, it was to drop him some food, talk for a few minutes then let him get back to work. But he could tell this would not be one of those happy visits.

"Helena. Anna. What are you doing here?"

"John, we need to go somewhere and talk."

He looked at Anna and knew this wasn't going to be good.

~

"How dare you tell the kids about the lawyer?" she said in that stern voice that could terrify anyone who was on the receiving end of it.

"Are you kidding me? Think how ridiculous that sounds? How dare you do this to our family? Even if you no longer see Gina as our family that baby is."

"That's why I'm doing this."

"No, it's not. You are doing this to get back at her. I've stood by you before Helena but not this time. The kids and I are done. We aren't helping you do this. And we're not shutting her out. You want to do it fine but we're not joining you. I have to get back to work. Anna, take your mother home."

The first few minutes in the car were pure silence. Anna didn't dare turn on the radio as she didn't want her choice of music to give her mother anything else to complain about.

"Anna, I can't believe you all are turning against me."

"That's where you are wrong. We just aren't standing with you this time. It's not right and we just can't do it. I'm really just praying eventually you will see that."

~

"What did she say after that?" asked Christian, looking at Anna who was stretched out on his couch with a glass of merlot in her hand.

"Nothing. A few minutes later we were home and

she just got out of the car and left."

"That's not really like her."

"Tell me about it. Who knows what she will do next but it probably involves going to see Gina?"

"I will talk to her," said Christian, as he picked up his phone and sent Gina a text asking if he could come over.

~

Gina opened the door with her dark hair flowing freely on her shoulders, a hint of lipstick on her mouth, and Christian thought she still looked beautiful, despite everything she was going through.

"Come in, Christian," she said politely, a big difference from when the two always greeted each other with an embrace no matter how often they were together. And a far cry from when she lay crying on his and Anna's shoulders the other night.

"Thanks. How are you? How is the baby?"

"We are good."

When Gina didn't attempt to fill the silence, Christian just came out with it. "She went back to the lawyer. I thought you should be prepared."

"I know. He served me the papers and I was ready with my own response."

"So, you did go see a lawyer. Good for you, Gina."

Her shoulders started to relax a little and she moved over to the couch and gestured for him to sit down.

"Thank you for warning me. This is not something I wanted to do but you were right. I had to be ready. My only hope is that it doesn't move past this stage. I just hope the lawyer told her to drop it."

"I honestly don't know the answer to that. But even if he did, you know my mother doesn't drop anything."

"I'm well aware."

"So, what are you going to do now?"

"Pray."

"And what else?"

"That's it, Christian. It's only been a month since I truly started pulling myself together. In two months, I have a baby coming. I think I have other things I need to figure out. I did what I needed to do and now the next move is up to her."

"What can I do to help?"

"Pray."

"You know that's not me, Gina."

"I don't know what to tell you, Christian. Prayers are what I need right now. Prayers that your mother will back off."

"Let's just say she did. That she decided to call all this off with the lawyers. Would you let her back in your life?"

"In an instant."

"You really are the most amazing person you know that?"

"It's not me, Christian. It's God."

"I'll call you next week," and he did something he hadn't done since before Alex died. He leaned over and kissed her on the cheek and walked out the door.

~

Christian walked into Nick's, the local bar not far from his house, badly needing a drink. Apparently so did his dad as he spotted him hunched over a pint of lager.

"Hey, old man, what's up," said Alex trying to mask everything that was really going on in his head that he didn't want to share.

"Hey, Christian, I had to get out of that house."

"What did Mom do now?"

"Well apparently you drove her to the lawyers' office today."

"Dad, I didn't know I was dropping her there. I have no idea what happened after that."

"Yeah, I figured."

"Well Gina had a response all ready to Helena's legal claim and your mother is none too happy."

"I can't imagine she is."

"The lawyer told her she should drop it."

"And?"

"Come on. We both know your mother doesn't drop anything."

"Yup, that's what I just told Gina."

"This really makes me sick. I am still grieving my son and my granddaughter. This could be a time when this baby helps us heal. Why can't she see that?"

"Because Mom has to be in control."

"As bad as everything your mother is doing is, "I'm more worried about Gina's health and mental state."

"Why?"

"Christian. Gina is still grieving. She is going through all this while pregnant and hasn't exactly been taking the best care of herself. I think this could be the thing that saves her. We have to keep her healthy so she can actually deliver a perfect child."

He didn't mention the gun. No one else needed to know about that. He knew Christian wouldn't say anything to Helena willingly but he didn't want to take any chances of it slipping out. That would be all Helena needed to go back to the lawyer with.

Christian signaled to the bartender who knew him

well.

"Your regular beer?"

"No give me a whiskey straight up."

"That kind of day?"

"You have no idea."

TARA TAFFERA

Chapter 12

"Gina," her mother gushed. "You look amazing," she said, as she enveloped her in a huge hug.

"Thanks, Mom."

"Come here, Gina," said her Dad as he drew her in for an embrace as well. "How's that baby doing?"

"Great. Let's go in and get seated though before I tell you more. I'm starving."

After Gina had polished off a large serving of stuffed shells, a salad and garlic bread, her mother couldn't have been happier. She couldn't help but think back to when her daughter went days without eating.

"I'm so glad you agreed to meet us halfway, Gina. It is so good to see you. Though this may be the last time we can do this. I can't have you driving as you get closer to your due date."

"You and Dad will just have to visit and help me get ready for the baby."

"Of course, we would love to."

"Great. Elizabeth and I are going to start packing

90

away some things ..."

Her mother took her hand. "I know that will be hard."

"It will ... But listen it has been so great to see you and I know you are so thrilled that I am getting my act together. Thanks for hanging in there with me by the way."

"Gina, stop," said her father. "That's what we do."

"I know. So, I hate to bring up bad news but I really need to tell you something."

~

She finished her story about Helena and the lawyers about five minutes ago and was now alone with her mother. Her father was so enraged he had to leave the restaurant. Her mother had said next to nothing. She only asked Gina questions she couldn't answer then stopped talking altogether. They looked over to the door and saw Sal walk back in, a hundred times more composed than before, then slid into the seat almost like nothing had happened.

"I'm sorry, Gina. I just had to process that, and I needed to take a walk."

"I know, Dad. Believe me I am still processing."

She almost choked on her water when she saw a few tears emerging from his eyes.

"Dad?"

"I'm just so proud of you, Gina. When I think of how far you have come and how you are handling all this."

"Thanks, Dad. I wouldn't still be here if it weren't for the two of you. You are the only ones who stuck by me. Well, you and Elizabeth."

"So, what's your next move?"

"I'm just waiting to see what Helena says about my response to her papers. She has been silent."

"Maybe she ..." her Mom started then stopped.

They all knew what she was thinking wasn't true. Gina would be hearing from her soon. What the message would be she didn't know.

~

Gina walked into the grief group dressed in sweats and a comfy sweatshirt—though the top she chose almost made it impossible for her to get here. It had been more than seven months but when she pulled Alex's favorite NYPD sweatshirt over her head, and smelled his scent, she had to sit down on the bed and let the tears flow. The old Gina from a few months ago would have stayed there feeling sorry for herself. But today she knew she had to get to the meeting. She walked in and was actually pleased to see a seat open next to Grace. The woman waved and motioned for her to come over and pulled her into an embrace.

"How are you doing, dear?"

"I'm hanging in there. It's been a rough day but I have to say I am proud I made it here tonight."

"Well, I'm proud of you too, Gina. Most of the time that's the hardest part."

"Hello everyone," Dr. Roberts interrupted. "Let's all take a seat and get started. Now let's join hands and start with a word of prayer."

"Dear, Lord," she started. "Thank you for getting everyone here safely tonight. May you be at the center of this meeting and allow those present to speak freely and share their feelings, their grief, their pain, all without judgment. Above all else, let them know that you are here with them to help them heal. Be with us tonight. In your name we pray. Amen."

"Amen," said the 15 or so people in attendance.

"Does anyone want to share something positive that happened to them this week? Remember it's the smallest things you get through that can help give encouragement to others."

"I will," said the slender man wearing all black, sitting near the door.

Gina hadn't seen him before but that didn't say much considering she had only been here a few times and had never spoken to anyone. She had been running in and out, almost to check the grief-meeting box but not open herself up to others. She hadn't wanted to hear about their pain. She had enough going on. But today she seemed eager to hear what he would say. What was his story?

"Well, as many of you know, my five-year-old son died last year after drowning in a swimming pool. My wife has never been to a meeting with me. She resents that I come, that I pray to the same God who took her son away. Tonight, when I was leaving she told me she hoped it would help me. She has never said that before. I asked her if she wanted to come and she answered, 'Ask me another time. Maybe I will.'"

He stopped to wipe a few tears from his eyes and Gina had a few she was forcing away just from listening to his story.

"Thanks for sharing," said Dr. Roberts. "We can all take comfort from this small milestone and will pray that your wife may take you up on your offer. And if she doesn't, she knows that you are always there for her."

"Amen," uttered Grace softly.

"Anyone else?"

"I will," Gina heard herself say. "As most of you know I have never really shared my full story. I lost my husband and child 7 months ago in a car accident. My mother-in-law and her family—who were also my family--disowned me as the mother-in-law blames me for the accident. The other members have since come back into my life and that is hopeful. You can probably see that I am seven months pregnant. This baby is what got me out of the mind-numbing pain about a month ago. Before that I wasn't taking care of myself one bit—so much so that my mother-in-law is going to court to get custody of the baby."

A collective sigh went through the room but Gina continued.

"Yeah, I know. Tell me about it," she nervously joked. "As bad as all that is I have learned I need to move forward and am relying on God. But my good news for this week is simply getting here tonight. I didn't want to come. I cried right up until when I pulled into the parking lot. But I needed to be here."

"Thanks for sharing, Gina. I know that was so hard and just know that we are here for you on your timetable. And most importantly God is here for you."

"Thank you."

When the meeting ended Gina wasn't able to escape as she normally did in the past. But tonight, she didn't mind as about four people came up just to tell her they were proud of her. That's it. They didn't push. They just put their hand softly on her back and whispered words of encouragement.

Just maybe she could do this. Before driving away from the meeting, she looked at her phone and saw a text from Christian.

"Ice cream? Our spot?"

"Tonight?"

"Why not?"

"Meet you there in ten minutes?"

"See you there."

~

Gina slid into the red leather seat at The Creamery and couldn't help staring at Christian.

"What's wrong?" he asked concerned when she wouldn't speak.

"Nothing."

"Gina."

"Christian. Don't push."

She couldn't tell him that sometimes when she looked at him he took her breath away. He just resembled Alex so much, especially tonight in his white cotton button up that she could tell was untucked from his jeans just like Alex wore it. Thankfully, the waitress saved her when she came over.

"Gina! It's so nice to see you." Then her eyes moved down to her stomach. Even though the booth was hiding part of her body these days it was pretty evident there was a baby in there.

"Are you?"

"I am."

Then the silence as she mentally did some calculations and deduced it was likely Gina's dead husband's baby.

"I'll have the hot fudge sundae."

"The works?

"You know it."

Christian could tell something was wrong from the

minute she walked in and her smile faded when she saw him but he was struggling to figure out why. The comment from the waitress didn't make things any better.

"How was your night?" Christian offered.

"It was good. I was at the grief group."

"Want to talk about it?"

"Not really. But I think it's helping. I just need to keep going."

"Do people ever take family members with them?"

"Sometimes."

"Could I go with you next time?"

"Can I think about it?"

"Sure."

Then their ice cream came, and Gina drowned her worries in her bowl, not wanting to look at Christian a minute longer than she had to, or think about all the times they used to spend together, even without Alex, talking and laughing. It would be so easy to go back there but then again so much had happened. He really hurt her, and she didn't know what to do with all these feelings. But most of all she wondered what he was thinking. Was he just with her out of a sense of obligation to Alex? Would things ever go back to the way they were—when it was so easy for them to be together—when they could talk about anything? It was easier to just eat her ice cream in silence.

Chapter 13

"You ready for this?" asked Elizabeth as Gina opened the door.

Gina looked her friend over who was dressed in gray sweats, a pink sweatshirt and her blonde hair was pulled up in a messy bun on her head. She was ready to work. Gina glanced past Elizabeth and saw her car door open and empty boxes piled on the driveway.

"I am but maybe not as much as you."

"Hey, all you have to do is listen to everything I say. I have a plan. We are going to make so much progress today."

"Gee, that sounds so fun."

"You will be happy when you have a nursery ready for that baby boy."

"We are going to get it all done today?"

"Well, I called in some reinforcements to come later to help us."

Gina raised an eyebrow.

"Come on, Gina. I hope you don't mind. I know

you are trying to make peace with Anna and Christian, so I invited them later to help. They really wanted to."

"Don't apologize--its fine. I just don't want to lose it around them. It's not like it was with them and I'm not ready to let them see how much I am hurting."

"I know. Just don't hide anything from me okay. I am here for you. Whatever you need I will help you through this today."

"Thanks, Elizabeth. I don't know what I would do without you."

Her friend hugged her then let go, eager to get started. "Wait until you hear the playlists I made for us!"

~

An hour later they were sitting in Teresa's room surrounded by all her clothes since from birth to age 2, with Mercy Me playing in the background. The clothes that weren't pulled out of her drawers were taken out of the closet where Gina had them stacked and labeled in bins. They had sorted them all so the ones Gina's boy would be able to wear were all organized by age waiting for his arrival.

Gina didn't let on to Elizabeth but all she could do was think about the pile of Teresa's clothes in the corner. Maybe she did know because just then she started quietly packing them neatly in the storage boxes she brought along. Gina just sat there and watched.

"Where do you want these, Gina?"

"We can't get rid of them."

"We don't have to. Want me to take them downstairs in your basement?"

She just nodded.

~

"Gina. They will be here any minute. They are bringing take out. I figured we will get some food before we start up again."

"What's next?"

"Adding some male touches to that room of course. Are you okay with that?"

"I am."

"We will leave the color. Luckily yellow goes either way. But they are bringing some decorations to put in there. Is that alright?"

She hugged her friend. "Yes, it's fine. I don't want you to have to tiptoe around me. I know we have to do this. It will help me move forward. I just couldn't do it without you."

"Luckily you don't have to."

And then the doorbell rang.

"Who wants Vinny's?" yelled Christian as he walked in the door.

"No!"

"Oh yes," said Anna as she helped carry in the bags.

"We know how much you love it there."

"I hope you brought lasagna and garlic bread."

"Do we know you or what?"

"Yes! You guys are the best."

~

"So, what have you accomplished today?" asked Christian as he grabbed the last piece of garlic bread.

"We organized the clothes," said Gina flatly. "We have a whole bunch of neutral outfits tucked away waiting for a baby boy."

"Well, wait until you see all the stuff we brought for his room," said Anna. "Christian lets go grab it all and start bringing it in."

While they headed for the car, Elizabeth cleared away the mess and watched Gina stare at the corner of the wall, as if she was dreading what was coming next.

"You okay, G?"

"Not really."

"Who's ready to decorate?" Anna sang out as she walked in with Christian carrying multiple bags of various sizes.

~

Gina looked at the cute little cowboy decorations scattered throughout the room. It really looked great but mostly Gina was just thrilled she didn't have to put an ounce of energy into dreaming up this décor.

"Gina, are you okay?" asked Christian as he sat down beside her while Anna and Elizabeth fiddled with some remaining decorations.

"And don't say you're fine."

"Then don't ask me."

Christian just looked at her surprised at what she had said.

"Sorry."

"Don't be."

"Would chocolate help?"

"Always."

"No, seriously."

"Seriously, Christian. All I see is Teresa in here. And I see Alex rocking her over in that chair. Hopefully all this heartache will fade in time but even with the new decorations I still just see them. I just want it to hurt a little less."

Anna and Elizabeth came over then, dropped the clothes in their hands and sat next to her. "We are here for you, Gina," said Anna.

"I know. Listen guys I am so grateful for everything you did here today. The room looks amazing. But it was a lot. I kind of want to be alone."

"Are you sure that's a good idea?" asked Elizabeth.

"Yes, I will be fine, really. You can text me later and check on me."

"You know I will."

"And we will too," said Christian.

"Seriously, please call us if you need us."

"I will."

~

When they left the house Anna looked at her phone and saw a text.

"Dad wants to know if we want to meet him at the bar."

"Sure."

~

They were on their second drink, wine for Anna, whiskey for the two men, while John was still feeling bad Gina was left all alone.

"I think you guys should go back over there."

"Dad, that is like the fifth time you have said that," said Christian. "What is wrong with you? She will be fine."

"Listen. I didn't want to tell you this but Gina had access to Alex's gun."

"Dad, how could you do that?" yelled Christian.

"Calm down. I took it back from her once I figured out how bad she was."

"Oh, you mean after it dawned on you that her husband and child were gone?" said Christian.

He looked at his sister. "Wait, why aren't you surprised by this? You knew?"

"I saw Dad right after it happened. It was the day I found about the baby."

Christian turned back to his father, forgetting about Anna's omission for now.

"That's why you were asking us so many questions tonight about her mental state," said Christian.

"Yes, I just can't get it out of my head. But I took it back. There is no way she could have gotten another one. She only wanted it because you know how nervous she gets."

"I'm leaving. Dad take Anna home," then he walked out the door texting Gina that he was coming back over.

She answered the door in her pajamas, the top snug on her bulging belly, with her hair in a messy ponytail with several tendrils emerging haphazardly. The TV was on and she had a cup of tea next to her chair.

"Why are you back, Christian? I'm fine. I'm just curled up with a good Hallmark movie and a cup of tea."

"Dad told me about the gun."

She didn't miss a beat, knowing this day would come.

"Oh, come on. I gave that back. And I took it for safety. That's it. Where are you going?" she screamed as he took off up her stairs.

"Christian, stop! There is nothing here."

"I need to see for myself. I need to know you are safe."

"What do you think I am going to do?" she screamed.

She couldn't take it anymore but she didn't have the energy to fight him. It had been 20 minutes and now he was going through all her kitchen cupboards and drawers.

"Christian. Please stop," she pled with tears streaming down her cheeks. "Just leave me alone."

"I'm sorry I didn't believe you. I had to be sure."

"Does Anna know?"

"She does."

"Are you going to tell your mother?"

"Gina, how could you even ask me that?"

"Because it's hard to trust anyone anymore."

"Even me?"

She didn't have to answer. He knew.

Gina woke up the next day and walked into Teresa's room just as she had every morning since the accident. She went to sit in the rocker as was her habit. All traces of Teresa were gone except for her baby blanket that Anna and Elizabeth had quietly left on the dresser. She walked over, put her cheek on its soft fabric, and never even made it to the rocker. She just fell in a heap on the floor and cried.

She decided she wasn't looking at her phone today. Maybe it was a good thing she didn't have a house line anymore. When she let that payment lapse, she never bothered getting it back. She took her cell, put it in Teresa's room, wondering if there would ever be a time she didn't call it that, and shut the door behind her.

~

Christian and Anna gathered at their parents' house every Sunday for dinner and today was no different. Except that it was because the siblings, along with their Dad, just couldn't get over what Helena was doing to Gina.

After everyone piled their plates with grape leaves

stuffed with rice, moussaka, and Greek salad they all sat down around the mahogany round table.

"So, what did you two do yesterday," Helena asked her children.

They exchanged glances.

"We went to Gina's and helped her and Elizabeth decorate the nursery."

Their mother stiffened.

"Does she know the sex yet?"

"Mom, it's a boy," said Anna, hoping her mother would get a little excited.

A tear ran down her cheek and she left the table.

"What should we do, Dad?"

"Don't worry about it. You guys stay here. I will go talk to her."

"Christian, have you talked to Gina today?

"No, and I called her and sent her like five texts."

"I called her twice and texted her too."

"Maybe I should go over there."

"Christian, if she is ignoring us it's likely for a reason. We can't expect her to just pick up where we left off and not remember that we cut her off all that time."

"You are right. Yesterday was great but she can't just flip the switch and forget everything we did to her."

"Agree. But I'm texting Elizabeth. I'm still worried and need to know she is okay."

She had a response not a minute later. "She's not responding to Elizabeth either. But she thinks she should give her space." They both just looked at each other.

"I know, Bro. It's not your strong point but you have to do it."

~

John cracked the door and saw Helena sitting on the bed crying.

"It's a boy, John," she whispered when she saw him.

"It really is a blessing you know."

"I know. But I just want him to be well cared for and I don't think she can do that."

There goes the reconciliation.

"Helena, how would you know? You haven't seen her. You haven't called her. You haven't asked us or the kids about her. You just know the past. We told you she is getting better and you haven't cared to ask more."

"Fine, how is she?"

"Let's go ask the kids."

~

"Christian. Anna. Don't go yet," Helena said, as she saw them grabbing their coats.

"What's up, Mom?"

"Tell me about Gina."

Anna answered first. "It's tough for her. Just like it is for you—for all of us. Before she could barely get out of bed, but she is now taking care of herself and preparing for the baby. Ask Christian--you know he has always been super close to her and is good at figuring out what's going on in her head."

Helena looked at her son. "So?"

"It's like Anna said, the fact that she is functioning is progress. I see this baby as a miracle for that and many other reasons. But she still has a lot of work to do. And she desperately needs the people around her to let her know they are there for her."

Helena ignored that comment and Anna continued.

"She is going to a grief group and Christian said she is finally starting to open up there so that's good."

Helena stayed silent again and wondered just how much time her son was spending with the woman who killed her family.

~

"So what do you think?" asked Anna as they drove away.

"She's not ready to forgive. It's all over her face."

"I know."

"We really have to watch what we say, Anna. I know we love Mom but she is not beyond using things we tell her for her own purposes."

"You are right though I wish you weren't."

"Maybe we should listen to Gina. I'm starting to think God is the only one who can heal this situation."

Christian glanced over at her, surprised as his sister never talked about taking problems to God.

"You might be right."

~

Gina looked at the clock. It was seven already. She had spent all day sitting in front of the TV, switching between junk food and some actual nutrition.

She knew she couldn't avoid it any longer. She walked up to Teresa's room to try so see it in a new light. She saw her cell phone in a corner on the floor where she left it and still made no move toward it. Toward the people who would be asking her all the questions about how she was doing. She looked over at the dresser with the cowboys dotting the surface and wondered where Elizabeth had put the dolls that were here just yesterday. She noticed the new blue curtains—

when had her friend done that? She honestly had no idea when that happened. Was she really here yesterday or in a fog? She looked at the chair and tried to picture herself rocking baby Alex. But the image didn't come. She looked at the phone on the floor and left the room.

Chapter 14

This Monday was a far cry from the last one where she could barely get herself to grief group. Today she was almost looking forward to it, as she had a lot of feelings to process and was hoping the people there could help. She was in what was becoming her normal seat next to Grace, the sharing was complete, and it was time for the part Gina was actually looking forward to.

"Who has something they want to discuss tonight?" asked Dr. Roberts.

Gina raised her hand, and the group didn't seem as shocked as last week.

"When do the images stop?"

"What do you mean, Gina?"

"I mean, everywhere I look I see them. This weekend my friends helped me get the baby's room ready. It was my daughter's room. It looks different but still I walk in there and all I see is her. All I see is Alex and I in there together taking care of her. When does that stop?"

"It doesn't," said a man in his fifties. Gina thought his wife died but she couldn't remember for sure.

"How can it not?"

"It lessens," said Grace. "You still see these images. But in a few months, you will have new ones mixed in. Of you rocking your new baby boy. Of you and your friends in there helping you. You will still see those you lost but they won't be as painful as they are today."

"And with time you may even look on those memories and images with joy that you had those moments," said the man.

"Thank you."

"Thank you, Gina for sharing," added Dr. Roberts. "This is a good time for me to tell you about something new we are doing next week. Gina, this may be a little rough for you—it will be tough for many of you. But the process works, and I really hope you give it a chance. Next week I want all of you who have someone in your life come to this meeting with you."

Gina visibly cringed when she heard it.

"It can be someone also affected by this loss. Or it can be a person who has seen you through this difficult time. But it's an important part of moving forward so I really need you to push past your discomfort and do this with me."

Gina was pretty sure she would be sick next week.

Two days after grief group Gina could not stop thinking about the meeting. How was she going to move forward if she didn't follow what was being asked of her? These people knew what they were doing right? She really hoped so, then picked up the phone to call Elizabeth.

"Gina, I feel awful," Elizabeth said for the third

time.

"Stop, its fine really. You have to go on that work trip. I get it I really do."

"I mean if I wasn't presenting…"

"Elizabeth, stop. It would have been great if you were here but it will be okay."

"What about your Mom?"

"I thought of that. Now that I am getting stronger things are so much better between us. We talk a lot. But she wants me to tell her stuff and I honestly don't know if she can handle it all. I am her daughter. She doesn't like to see me in pain."

"Sadly, I think you are right."

"What about Christian?"

"Yeah, I thought of him too."

"What's stopping you?"

"Everything. Depending on someone I want to trust but who hurt me. Depending on someone who by the way makes me think of Alex every single time I look at him."

"Have you thought about Anna?"

"I have. But even after everything I just said I know it should be Christian. He actually asked me a few weeks ago if he could go with me one time."

"Well, there you go."

"Yeah, I think you are right. I think it may help him as much as it helps me. Sometimes I forget he lost his brother—who was his best friend—and his niece that day."

~

She wrote the text, "Can I come over quick?" and hit send.

He texted back, "Absolutely."

After they had finished the small talk about their day she knew she had to do it.

"Listen, Christian I want to ask you something and it's really hard for me.

"Anything, Gina."

"Will you come to grief group with me next Monday?"

"Of course. I told you I would go with you."

"I know but this is different. This week she wants us to bring someone either close to us or who also feels our loss. Of course, you fit both of those. But I don't know what it is going to be like. I don't know if you have to share or ..."

"Stop."

"Stop what?"

"Worrying about others. I'm going to be there for you. It might be hard for me, yes, but that's not for you to worry about. I want to do this so you can continue to heal and be there for that baby of yours."

"Thank you."

~

Gina never felt so uneasy before her group. It was all she could think about from the time she woke up. She didn't like the unknown. She never did. She wished she knew more about what was going to happen tonight. And she really hoped she didn't fall apart in front of Christian. She wanted to be strong. She wanted him—and everyone in his family—to know she was going to be okay.

"You ready for this?" she asked before they walked in.

"I'm ready. Are you?"

"I am."

There was double the amount of people here tonight which made sense. She was glad it looked like everyone had someone to bring with them to help them through this. She saw Grace waving at them and two empty seats next to her.

"Hi, Grace. This is my brother-in-law Christian."

"A pleasure to meet you. This is my daughter Claire."

And then it dawned on her. Gina had been so wrapped up in her own problems she had no idea what loss Grace had suffered.

"It's nice to meet you, Claire," Gina said.

They sat down and Grace whispered in her ear. "Well isn't he is a handsome fella."

Gina whispered back. "He looks exactly like my husband."

Grace patted her hand, knowing how hard that must be.

"Thank you so much for everyone who came to help one of your loved ones and perhaps do some healing of your own. To get started, I need a brave pair to be my first guinea pig."

"I can do all things through Christ who strengthens me," Gina said silently to herself before she looked at Christian, saw his approval then raised her hand.

"Thank you, Gina. Tell me who you brought with you."

"This is Christian. Alex's brother. And my friend."

They all nodded knowing the hurt he was going through as well.

"Christian, why did you want to come here tonight?"

"Because Gina is my family. I want to be there for

her. I don't know how much she has shared here but we were really close. Then when my brother died my Mom blamed Gina for everything, and we all took our Mom's side. I'm not making excuses but I think we were just all blinded by grief and didn't want to say anything that would upset our mother further. I think about it every single day and can't get rid of that guilt."

"You need to, Christian," said Dr. Roberts. "Keeping hold of that isn't helping either of you. Have you asked Gina to forgive you?"

"He has," Gina interjected.

"And did you?"

"I have."

"Well, that's the hardest part. So, do you talk about your loss together?"

"We don't," answered Christian. "And I want to. But I know she is so hurt that I don't want to make it worse."

"Do you want to talk about it, Gina?"

"Yes. The three of us had so many great times. I want to remember the happy memories. I want to talk about him but I am afraid."

"Of what?"

"Of crying every time. I don't know. Of thinking I won't get better if I dwell on the past."

"Gina, it's all part of moving forward. Talking about memories will do wonders for your healing process."

"Will both of you promise to remember what I said and do some sharing this week?'

"We will," they both said in unison.

~

They were almost at Christian's house and he

finally broke the silence.

"Thank you for taking me, Gina. It was hard but I am glad I went."

"Me too. I'm glad I asked you."

"So we are going to do what she said right?"

"Right, just not tonight. I'm mentally beat."

"Me too," he said as she pulled into his driveway.

"I'll call you this week," then he leaned over, kissed her on the cheek and walked toward the house.

~

"So how was it?" Elizabeth asked when Gina picked up the phone the next day.

"Easy actually."

"Really?"

"Yes, but the hard part is what's coming next."

"What do you mean?"

"She said we have to talk about Alex. Doing that will help us heal."

"Wow."

"I know."

"She's right though. If you fall apart it's okay."

"I know. I just feel like I am finally putting myself together. The fact that I can leave the house and go to that group is huge. I'm afraid if I talk about everything, I'm going to lose it again."

"You will cry, Gina. It will be hard. You may want to stop. But you have come too far. I know you can get through this."

"Thanks. I don't know what I would do without you. And speaking of that, I am only five weeks away from my due date. I am terrified, and that's why you are the only one I want in there with me. Will you do it?"

"I would be honored," she said fighting back tears.

~

"I'm coming over with dinner tonight," read the text. "Hungry for anything special?"

"Nope, you decide."

"See you at six."

~

Gina opened the door in what appeared to be her usual attire now. A pair of sweats, a comfy cotton shirt and her hair piled up in a bun and no makeup. Not that she needed it.

"Hey, Gina."

"Hey, Christian, thanks for bringing the food."

"No problem."

They sat and enjoyed their dinner speaking hardly at all.

"G?"

She looked up from her baked ziti. "This doesn't have to be weird you know."

"I know. I felt like things were getting better but now that we have this pressure on us I feel like I just went ten steps back with you. I'm sorry."

"Don't be. I know how you feel. Can I ask you a question?"

"Sure."

"Why do you have a hard time looking at me? I notice it every time I see you."

She arched her eyebrows and gave him that sarcastic look.

"What? I really don't know."

"Guys really are clueless. Christian, you look exactly like him."

"You're right. I didn't have a clue. I don't know what to say."

"I'm sorry if I made you uncomfortable. In time I will get over it but sometimes the memories are just too much."

"What do you miss most about him?"

She blushed.

"When he would come up behind me every morning, hug me and tell me I am the most beautiful woman in the world. When I would walk in the room and see him rocking Teresa and his look of pure love. Just being with him, talking to him. I miss what we had."

"I want to find that someday. I was always in awe of you two."

"What about you?"

"Hanging out with him at my apartment, watching the Florida Seminoles play. Talking smack. Just being with my brother."

"What else?"

"All of us being together as a family on Sundays."

"I miss that too."

"I'm sorry."

"Don't be."

"She's my mother."

"It's okay, really. They are gone. We can't expect things to be the same. They never will be."

"Do you imagine the future when little Alex is here?"

"I don't."

He tried to hide the shock on his face. He couldn't imagine that would be good with a baby coming in a little over a month.

"Why?"

"Because I can't imagine doing this without Alex."

She was crying now so he went to her and took her in his arms while the tears continued to fall. Finally, he pulled back, and took her face in his hands.

"Gina. Alex would want me to remind you how strong you are. That you can do this. You take it one day at a time and you will succeed. You know that, right?"

More tears came.

"I'm botching this," he said as he dropped his hands and pulled away.

She grabbed his hand back. "Christian, you're not. Feel this," she said as she took his hand and moved it to her belly. "That's your nephew."

"Wow," was all he could say as now he fought back tears.

"Christian, you can cry too you know. You don't have to stay strong for me. Dr. Roberts said we both have to heal. I want to be there for you too."

"Alex was really lucky to have you. And so was Teresa. You are going to be an amazing Mom to your little boy. And your parents, Elizabeth, me, Anna. We are all going to be here for you. Whatever you need."

"Promise?"

"Forever."

"Thanks for coming over tonight."

"You're welcome. But I have to ask you something else. Can you do this with Anna too? She really misses you. She wants to reach out but she is afraid. She always tells me she doesn't want to make things harder for you."

"I miss her too. Tell her to text me this week and we will have a girl's night."

"She will love that."

"Gina, I know it's late but there is something I need to apologize for before I leave."

"It's okay, Christian."

"It's not. I was just worried for you and that's why I stormed in here looking for a gun."

"You just wanted to make sure I was safe. I need people like that around me and I'm thankful for it. Let's let it go."

"Are you sure?"

"I am. That's what family is for right?"

"Right. But I want you to know I trust you."

"I know that. And I'm starting to trust you again too."

And the tears started to fall again.

"Now who's the big baby?" she teased as he wiped his eye and she pulled him in for a hug.

~

"So how did it go?"

It was Sunday dinner, and the two siblings were hiding out from their mother again like a couple of little kids. They were in the hallway off the dining room as she finished getting everything on the table. They knew it was ridiculous but she didn't give them any choice.

"It was great," said Christian. "In fact, she wants to get together with you too."

"I know. We're actually hanging out tonight after I leave here. A girls' night with some cheesy movies and junk food."

"Awesome," he said, happy for his sister but a little jealous.

"What is it? Is she okay?"

"There is just one thing that worries me if you can maybe talk to her about it. She told me she doesn't think about what's going to happen when the baby is here."

"What do you mean?"

"She says she doesn't think about it because it's too hard. Her due date is five weeks away now. Is it me or is that a little weird? Isn't that what girls do? Overthink things?"

She jabbed him in the arm.

"None of this is normal. I don't know how she is supposed to act. I'm glad she is going to that group. I don't know that once a week is enough but I guess we were all happy she is doing that."

"She has the nursery together, and she asked Elizabeth to be there during the delivery. You are right. I'm not going to worry about that. We just need to stay a constant in her life. Between, Elizabeth, us and her parents we will make sure she has everything she needs."

Helena, listening from the other room, stepped back to the kitchen and informed John to tell the kids it was time for dinner.

Chapter 15

"So, what do you think? Helena asked her new lawyer, with an air of confidence.

"I still don't think you have a case Mrs. Andros," he said as he put down his notebook and pen, signifying the conversation was coming to an end.

"But."

"But, nothing. You want me to file a case because you heard she doesn't sit in her new baby's room and think about what it will be like when he arrives? I suggest you make amends if you want to be a part of this child's life."

Before he could say more, she picked up her purse, and stomped out the door. She then stood outside the building waiting for her first-ever Uber. She had run out of people to call and excuses to make.

~

"Dad, we have got to stop meeting here. People are going to talk," joked Christian as he patted his father on the shoulder and took the empty bar stool next to him.

Christian looked at his Dad and wondered when those wrinkles and deep bags under his eyes had appeared. The accident, his mother's antics, he could really tell the toll it was taking on his father.

"Hey, Christian. It's good to see you," he said simply before taking another pull of his beer.

"What did she do now?"

"I don't know and that's worse than anything."

Christian signaled at the bartender, pointed at his dad's glass to signify he wanted an ale then settled in for the latest family drama.

"What do you mean?"

"She was in a foul mood today."

Christian raised his eyebrows.

"No really. Worse than normal."

"What do you think it was?"

"Well, I got an email receipt telling me your mother took an Uber today." Christian nearly choked on his beer.

"I know, right? I wish I could have seen that one. I looked up the address and she was picked up at another law office."

"Dad!"

"I know but calm down. Judging from her bad attitude I'm just praying this lawyer gave her the same advice as the last one. Maybe now she will leave it alone."

"Maybe, but I think you are going to go through hell in the process."

"Tell me something I don't know, kid," then he signaled to the bartender to bring another round.

~

Gina was excited but nervous about Anna coming

over. They used to do these girls' nights at least once a week, even if Alex did join them more often than not after Teresa came. But once she started fussing, he always whisked her away so the girls wouldn't miss a second of their chick flick.

This was the first time they were doing this since the accident and that made Gina jumpy. In the past that's when she would have taken a drink. Tonight, she planned to stress eat as soon as Anna arrived.

The doorbell rang and when Gina answered it she could barely see her sister-in-law past the groceries hiding her face.

"What, did you buy out the store?"

"Well, I told you I was bringing the snacks."

"For a month?"

Anna laughed and remembered how much she missed Gina. She was so nervous about how this would go. She didn't know if Gina had cravings now so she just bought all her favorites, just praying that this night would go well and help bring the two of them closer together.

"Sorry. You know how I get."

"I'm teasing, Anna. Heck I will probably eat half of it tonight. I'm starving."

Anna laughed and they started ripping open the bags, taking off the lids and setting up their very own smorgasbord when Gina stopped and touched Anna's hand.

"What's wrong?"

"Nothing, but it brings back memories. Good ones."

"I know. The last time we did this it was us, Teresa and Alex. Do you remember how she looked so amazed at all the food? She didn't know what chip to grab first."

"I know. I kept thinking about that today."

"Me too," said Anna as she squeezed her hand. "Do you know how amazed I am by you?"

"What?"

"Really, Gina. Look at everything you have gone through and here you are powering through it all."

"Is that what I am doing?"

"Yes. I don't mean to dredge up the past but you need to know how strong you are that you are bringing yourself out of all that. I don't know that everyone could handle this like you are. I don't know that I could."

"I didn't always know that I would."

Anna patted her on the arm. "I know and it's okay."

"It's not but thankfully I finally realized I needed to rely on the Lord. I am definitely not the one getting me through this. It's all Him. I only wish I had asked for some help earlier."

"Would you do something for me? I've been thinking about it a lot lately. Can we pray for my Mom?"

"Of course, but you don't need me for that."

"Oh my gosh, Gina, I am so sorry. How could I be so dumb to ask you that?"

"It's not that. I would be happy to pray with you. But you can talk to God too you know."

"I know. Can you do it tonight and then I will try to pray for her another time?"

Gina bowed her head and took Anna's hand.

"Dear, Lord. We thank you for all you have done for us. For this baby that will hopefully help this family heal. For Anna, Christian and I finding our way back to each other. I ask that you soften Helena's heart so she can see that we all want her to be a part of this baby's life. That we want to be a family again."

Anna opened her eyes. "You really want that? How can you forgive her?"

"I have to. It's what God asks of us. But honestly, Anna even I wonder if she will ask for it."

"I'm so sorry if I upset you."

"You didn't. I'm glad you asked me to do that. Let's do it more often when we are together."

"Which will be a lot right?"

"Yes!

"Gina, can I pray now? I need the practice."

"I would love that."

She took Gina's hand. "Dear, Lord. Thank you so much for Gina and please help her as she prepares to give birth to her precious baby boy. We know she will have some bad days but have her always remember to rely on you and that you will get her through it. And help her to always know that we are always here for her. Amen."

"That was beautiful. I'm amazed by you, Anna. I'm so glad you came back into my life."

"Me too. Listen Christian and I were talking, and we want to take you out for dinner one night. I know we all love eating takeout here but I think it's time to get out of the house."

"I don't know."

"Gina, you are doing so much better but you have to start getting out besides grief group and the occasional ice cream at The Creamery."

"That's exactly why I don't want to go out."

"What do you mean?"

"When Christian and I went there the waitress was all weird. You could tell she thought I was the sad widow, then she looked at my stomach and didn't even try to hide her unease at the situation."

"But you can't just stay inside."

"Why can't I? I go to my doctor appointments, to grief group. The grocery store. Oh wait, that didn't work out so well once either."

"Gina, I am sorry," said Anna, knowing she had pushed too far.

"I love you but you need to back off."

"I'm sorry. Here let me help you put all the food away."

"It's fine. I got it."

Anna knew better than to think she would change her mind. She closed the space between them, gave her a hug and walked out the door feeling terrible that she had ruined their night.

~

"It was awful, Christian," said Anna, as she had driven straight to his house after leaving Gina's. "We had so much fun, we even prayed together and then it ended so badly."

"Wait, you prayed?"

"Come on, Christian it's not like I'm an atheist."

"I know, I'm just surprised."

"Well, it's the only thing I know how to do. If Mom is going to welcome Gina back in the family God is the only one who can make that happen."

"You might be right."

"And now that I offended Gina, I need to pray she will forgive me. And I'm really worried about her. She can't just leave the house for the necessities. What happens when the baby comes? Is she never going to take him anywhere? To the park? For a walk."

"Calm down, Anna," but she was starting to make him worry. He remembered how that waitress just looking at her made Gina uncomfortable. What if she had to deal with that all the time?

"Christian?"

"I'm just thinking that you might be right. I have to figure out how to handle this. Maybe I can go to her grief group again and get the leader aside and ask her to talk to Gina."

"That could backfire, and she could just get mad at you too."

"I know. But we have to do something."

"The one time you listen to me I wish I wasn't right."

He playfully punched her arm them pulled her in for a hug.

"We'll figure it out, sis."

"Well, we only have a few weeks to do it."

"But we can't upset her either. Stress won't be good for the baby or her."

"I know. Let's hope your plan works. Can you call her now and ask if you can go with her tomorrow?"

He punched her name into the phone and waited.

~

After the pleasant greetings they rode to the meeting in silence. Gina asked Christian a few questions when she picked him up but he was unusually quiet today. She didn't know it was because he kept running through his head how to get Dr. Roberts aside to talk to her about Gina's reluctance to leave the house. He needed some advice: does he leave her alone, push a little? He had no idea what to do. Apparently, God did because in the end Christian didn't have to do a thing.

After they started the meeting with a prayer, Dr. Roberts introduced the night's topic: the pitfalls of isolation. She started the group by asking everyone to raise their hands if they had ever cut themselves off from the world while enduring their pain. Every hand went up. She then asked who still did this two months after their tragedy. All the hands went up. Four months after? Half the hands went up. Six months after? About a quarter of the hands went up including Gina's. Hers was halfway raised just because Christian knew she was embarrassed. That it was almost unbearable for her to hold it up at all. But he knew Gina and she always told the truth.

"Now, I want a raise of hands from those of you who believe the isolation helps."

No one lifted their arms.

"Why don't you ask us if we are unsure if it helps?" said Gina.

"Fair point. Okay let's see a raise of hands."

They all went up.

"Thanks for asking that question, Gina. Because it's what I was going to get to tonight. We cut ourselves off because we don't want to talk about the pain. We don't want people to ask us about it. We don't want to go to the grocery store and get the looks. You know what I mean--the looks."

Everyone nodded and a few laughed.

"So, we think it's easier to sit at home. Perhaps we drink. Or we eat. Or smoke. Or binge watch TV. Or make ourselves even sadder by looking at all our happy friends on Facebook. Does this describe any of you?"

All the hands went up again.

"We all know we do this but today we are going to talk about how to stop the cycle. How we can step out slowly and get back into the world again. And not just for the things we have to do—like the doctor and the grocery store—but things we want to do. The walks in the park, or visiting the restaurants we love. Who wants to know how to do that?"

All the hands went up.

"I'm sure all of you are sick of your friends and family saying you have to get back out there. Who tell you to ignore the ugly people out there who make comments, who give you the looks. I'm here to tell you it's not that easy. But I'm going to give you strategies to make it happen. And I know we have people here who are slowly doing this already and I am hoping those here who fit that bill will share their stories."

"First, you pray," she went on. "It's the most important thing. Before you walk out the door you ask God to give you strength to get through it. That doesn't mean it's smooth sailing from there. You will encounter challenges but that's when you tell yourself silently that you are strong. And you can survive this. Who here has something they say to themselves when things get tough?"

Gina raised her hand immediately then said, "I can do all things through Christ who strengthens me."

"Does it help?"

"It does. Sometimes I say it multiple times a day."

"Do you say it before you leave the house or before you are putting yourself in a tough situation?"

She thought for a second. "I'm not sure. But then again I rarely leave the house."

"I don't think a lot of us do. We wait until the conflict arises and then it's almost too late. We are already in a panic and upset and then we just want to flee back to our safe place of isolation."

They all seemed to think about that and nod their heads in unison.

"So, this week I want everyone to try it and I want you all to come back next week and share your experiences. Now it's not a magic bullet. But I will tell you that prepping yourself, steeling yourself up, putting God's armor around you, heading into the fray with your mind in the right place, will do wonders for getting yourself through the situation. And you have to keep doing it. It's the repetition, the falling down and getting back up again that will get you through. And I know all of you already know about that. Before long, you will be falling a lot less than before."

"But isn't it okay sometimes to want to be alone?" asked a younger woman in the group, who Gina remembered had lost her mother in a tragic car accident.

"Of course, it is. And I am glad you asked that. Sometimes you really do need time to yourself and it's very important that the people around you understand that. And I know that many do not. They are so worried about us that they crowd us every minute and sometimes that's what forces us into that isolation and makes the situation worse."

Everyone nodded their heads in agreement.

"That is where we have to be strong and speak up. We tell our family that we love them. That we know it's not good for us to be alone all the time but in some cases, we just need that to heal, and they can check on us but sometimes they have to give us some breathing room. Is anyone here good at doing that?"

Grace's hand went up. "Most of you know I lost my daughter almost two years ago in a brutal murder. Every day is still hard. But I was better a year after her death than I was in the few months after it. No one wanted to leave me for a minute, and I felt suffocated. They didn't mean it but they absolutely made it worse but I didn't know how to tell them that. So, I lashed out. I went further into isolation and it took me a few months to get out of it. I am still setting boundaries. My other two daughters continue to worry about me. They call me every day. They always want to come over. Believe me I love them for it but sometimes I just want to be alone with my grief and they respect that. But they don't let me go too long and I am so appreciative of them for it."

Gina squeezed Grace's hand and she went on.

"I want to share something else about this wonderful lady sitting next to me."

Gina was startled and looked over at her.

"We all get different looks from people. I get the looks of pity. It all comes from a good place but I just couldn't stand it. I hated leaving the house so I rarely did, and I know now that was the worst thing I could have done. I am sure Gina has it even worse. She gets the looks of pity then they probably look down at her stomach and give her a double dose. Am I right?"

All Gina could do was nod her head and fight back the tears. Christian took her other hand.

"How do you handle that Gina?" asked Dr. Roberts.

"I don't. I go where I need to and keep my head down. The one time I ventured out beyond the grocery store and the doctor, I got exactly that look and I haven't gone anywhere else since that wasn't essential."

"Will that change after what you heard here tonight?"

"Yes, I'm going to try to use the tools you gave us. I see a lot of 'I can do all things through Christ who strengthens me in my future.'"

They got in the car and Gina looked over at Christian. "Ice cream?"

"Do you even have to ask?"

That's all they said to each other the rest of the way there.

The same waitress came over to take their order and Gina was ready.

"Hi, Christian. Hi, Gina? How are you feeling?"

"I am great. Thank you for asking."

"Of course. I have been thinking of you a lot and hoping I would see you again.

Gina looked at her with surprise.

"I felt really bad about that first time you came in. I didn't mean to make you feel uncomfortable. I have felt really bad about it and wanted to apologize."

"It's forgotten," she replied.

"You are too kind. Are you guys getting the usual?"

"Same for me," said Christian.

"Me too," said Gina.

She returned with a hot fudge sundae for Christian and a caramel sundae for Gina which looked bigger than normal.

"I brought you an extra scoop," she said. "It's on me."

"Hey what about me?" asked Christian.

She just ignored him and walked away.

"So, what did you think of tonight's meeting?" asked Gina while diving into her ice cream with delight.

"I think it proves God is real."

She almost dropped her spoon.

"I'm serious. Anna and I have been worried about you and tonight I was freaking out trying to figure out how to get Dr. Roberts aside and ask her for some advice for how to help you and then that happened. If that's not God working, I don't know what is."

All Gina could do was nod and agree. Maybe good things really do come out of horrible situations.

"I'm really going to try, Christian. Tonight, really helped. And I am going to need you through this. And Anna. But when I need some space you have to give it to me."

"I promise. But you have to remember it's not going to be easy. You will fail and you just have to get back up and try again. Will you promise to do that for me?"

"I will."

"One more thing."

She looked at him with interest.

"I would say that Bible verse of yours twice if you ever run into my mother."

She laughed. "Valuable advice."

Then they went back to their ice cream and finished every bite.

~

Gina stood outside Teresa's room—she still thought of it that way, and said, "I can do all things through Christ who strengthens me," before opening the door.

She walked to the dresser and examined all the cute cowboy decorations Elizabeth and Anna had purchased and assembled there. She walked over to the crib and looked at the blue sheets with the little cowboy mobile above it. She turned the switch and listened to the familiar tune of "Rock a Bye Baby" and smiled. She moved over to the rocker and the blue blanket she had seen Elizabeth put there. When she unfolded it she saw the word Alex on it. She saw something very small in the corner and when she examined it she saw the words Alex Sr. (Dad) and Teresa (sister). She smiled thinking she had to call Elizabeth and thank her for being such a thoughtful friend. She sat down on the rocker holding the blanket up to her cheek and thought only of the baby in her stomach. Would he look like Alex? Teresa? What would it be like when he got here? Her life was going to completely change. It would no longer be just her and her grief. She felt hopeful for the first time in eight months. Immediately though Gina's type A tendencies kicked in. She didn't have any diapers, wipes. She mentally started a check list. "I guess I better start getting out of this house and getting ready for the baby."

~

"Hey, Elizabeth. I just wanted to tell you are the most amazing friend ever. I just looked at that blanket you put in the baby's room and I am so thankful for you. I love it. I also just realized how much stuff I need for this baby. Call me. We need to go shopping."

Elizabeth listened to the message then said, "Hey Anna. You need to come hear this." Then she played it again.

"Well, that makes me feel a little better because I am freaking out that this shower is a bad idea. But she just admitted she needs things so hopefully she will be happy."

"She will be. It's not like we are throwing this big thing. It's just us, her Mom, Grace, and a few other close friends. I think we are doing the right thing, and it will also help her start putting some of those things from her grief group into practice."

"You're right. Okay let's go over the plan again. Tomorrow she thinks the two of you are coming over here to have a girl's afternoon, right?"

"That's the plan. Don't worry. Look at this place. She is going to love it."

"You're right. Thanks, Anna."

~

Christian stood outside his parents' home and said Gina's verse before he walked in.

"Hey, Mom, hey, Dad."

"Hey son," said his Dad as he enveloped him in a hug.

"Where's your sister?"

"Hello to you too, Mom."

"Sorry, Christian, it's just you two always come together," then hastily kissed him on the cheek.

"She can't come today. Didn't she tell you?"

"No. Where is she?"

"She just had something today. I'm not sure," he said, thinking he wasn't going to be the one to endure his mother's wrath this whole afternoon just because Anna was afraid to tell their mother about the shower. She looked at him quizzically but shockingly she let it go and went back in the kitchen to prepare dinner.

His father came up to him and whispered, "So where is your sister?"

"At a baby shower for Gina."

"Good call on not mentioning that one."

134

"You're welcome. I didn't think the two of us would want to be at the receiving end of that anger today."

"So how is Gina?"

"She is good. You should really go see her you know."

Before he could answer, Helena walked in and announced that dinner was ready. While John was relieved he didn't have to answer his son, he knew Christian was right. Things had been difficult, and he and Helena just started getting back to some semblance of normal, and he didn't want to rock the boat. He knew that was a crummy move but he decided to just put off the inevitable a little longer.

~

"Bye, Mom. Thanks for dinner."

"You're welcome, Christian," she said as she kissed him on the cheek and sent him home with a bag of leftovers.

They watched him pull away and then she turned to John, "Get your coat. We're going to see Gina."

"Why?"

"Relax, John. I just want to go over there. I have a gift for the baby."

"She isn't home?"

"Where is she?"

"With Anna."

Helena took a breath trying to stay calm. "Anna missed our Sunday together to see Gina."

"I just found out today, Helena. And it's not like that. They are at an event together and happened to be scheduled for today."

"What's the event?"

"A baby shower."

"Well let's go then."

"No way."

"John, you take me or I get there myself."

"Helena, what are you doing? You hate her."

"I don't hate her."

"So, I imagined it when you said you wished she died instead of Alex and Teresa."

"No, you didn't." She walked over to the dining room chair and sat down.

"I'm glad you want to see her but crashing her baby shower probably isn't the right time or place."

"I wish you weren't so practical, John Andros."

He couldn't believe she had listened. Maybe the baby was making his wife's heart soften. But then he remembered Anna tell him she was praying for her mother. Maybe it was working.

~

Gina walked into Elizabeth's and saw about seven people, including her mother, standing in the foyer before they yelled, "Surprise!"

She turned to Anna and Elizabeth who looked terrified. "Thank you both for doing this. You don't have to look so scared. Let's go have a baby shower." Then she asked God for strength and walked over to her mother who enveloped her in a hug.

"This all looks amazing," said Gina, as she took in the decorations, a spread full of food that looked like it could feed 20 people, including cupcakes with blue icing and an A on top.

"Well, you two definitely know how to throw a shower. Thanks so much for doing this."

"You're welcome, Gina. We are glad you like it,"

said Elizabeth.

"But we aren't done yet," said Anna. "It's time for presents.

Gina had truly enjoyed this day. She felt at ease with everyone, though she knew they were all choosing their words wisely not wanting to upset her. But this is the part she was dreading since she walked in the door. When she had to sit in a chair with all eyes on her as she opened presents for a baby who didn't have a father, and a mother who was just taking it one day at a time.

"Okay," said Gina, as she sat where Elizabeth told her in the front of the room. She looked at the loving faces of her close family and friends. And Grace. She was excited that they invited her. This couldn't be easy for her. She had to sit here and look at Gina open presents for a baby and try not to think of her own daughter who would never have this experience. If she could do this then Gina could too.

Elizabeth handed her present after present, practical items that Gina really needed and was freaking out about the other day. Diapers, wipes, bottles … Gina was thrilled. Then it was over, and she saw her mother staring back at her with pity, and she turned away.

"Anna and Elizabeth, thank you so much for planning this. It was amazing. And thank you all for coming. I really had a lovely day."

People started to get up from their chairs and help clean up, grab their jackets and some leftover food. That's when her mother walked over. "How are you, honey?"

"I'm good, Mom. This really was a wonderful day. But you looking at me with pity isn't really helping."

"I just want to make sure you are okay."

"I am."

"Are you sad that *she* isn't here?"

"Mom, why are you doing this?"

Gina walked away to find Grace and say goodbye, but mainly to get away from her mother.

~

Maria watched with interest as Gina talked with Grace. She hadn't seen Gina laugh like that in a while. It made her sad that she and her daughter hadn't had a moment like that in ages. But she was her mother--the one who had to protect her. To make sure Gina was prepared for the storm that was to come. Yes, she had a beautiful baby on the way but her mother knew that things would not be easy and it was her job to make sure Gina was ready. That's why she had to be the one to hover. She couldn't be the fun one who planned the baby shower. Or the one who lost a child that she could grieve with. Little did she know she had a big job coming up in a manner of minutes.

~

Helena and John pulled up to Elizabeth's house. John felt like an idiot that he actually thought his wife would give up on this. He knew the gift was just an excuse. She couldn't stand that she was left out of this event and she just had to make an appearance.

"Helena, I am staying here. You can go inside and drop off your present. And if you want to tell Gina you are sorry that would be a great first step. We both know you aren't going to listen to me but I will be here waiting. Please show restraint."

~

Maria saw the black BMW pull up and knew who

was here but if she didn't see it she never would have believed it. She saw Helena step out of the car, and Maria ran toward the door, making a breezy comment about needing some air and no one really noticed as everyone was laughing and enjoying the day. She walked out to the car not wanting Helena to get any closer to the house.

"Helena, you can't be here."

"I'm just dropping off a gift, Maria."

"Fine, I will take it but you aren't going in."

"Will you tell her I'm sorry?"

Maria could feel the heat rising to her face and the words boiling to the surface but she wasn't going to be the one who ruined her daughter's day.

"I will tell her. Now please leave."

"Thank you, Maria," and she turned back toward the car, leaving John and Maria wondering how that happened so easily.

"Mom, where were you? Is that another present?"

"Yes, someone just dropped it off but I'm not sure who left it. You can look at it later."

Gina turned to go back to her guests and left the gift by the door, forgotten for now.

Everything had been cleared away and Gina sat in the plush couch at Elizabeth's, exhausted but happy. Her mother had started the drive home and Elizabeth and Anna were at the car putting all her gifts in the trunk.

"I'm going to follow you home, Gina," said Anna. "I can help you bring your gifts in and put them away for you."

She didn't even argue. She just smiled to show her thanks.

"Thank you so much for an amazing day. This was wonderful and I thank you for doing it for me."

"Anything for you, Gina. I love you."

"Love you too. Talk to you later."

~

Anna had brought all the gifts in the house and was putting them in the baby's room while Gina sat in the chair and watched under Anna's strict orders. There was only one gift left.

"Gina, this is the present that was dropped off. Here open it," she said as she walked over and handed it to her.

The wrapping was exquisite, a fact she didn't notice earlier with all the commotion of the baby shower. She didn't see a card anywhere, so she gently opened the paper. It was a photo of Alex, Teresa and Gina in a beautiful frame and an inscription read, "Welcome to the family, Alex. Your family loves you."

Gina dropped it on her lap as the tears came quickly.

"How beautiful. Who do you think?"

They looked at each other.

"Do you really think this was your mother? After everything she has done, she goes and extends this olive branch. She didn't have to include me in the photo but she did."

"Gina, I know you love my mother in spite of everything she has done, and I am amazed that you can do that. But you have to be careful."

"Anna, God doesn't put a timetable on forgiveness."

"Your faith amazes me. But we don't know what her plan is."

"Maybe she doesn't have a plan. Maybe she is ready to forgive me for what I did."

"For what you did? Gina, don't tell me you believe the lies she has been spewing about you being to blame for the accident."

"Why wouldn't I? She is right, isn't she? If I didn't plan that date, they would both be here now."

"I can't believe this. I had no idea you believed her."

"Well, then you never thought hard enough. How could some of what she has been saying not sink in? You don't think I'm human?"

"I can't believe my mother is ruining such a perfect day."

"She's not doing it, Anna. You are. You could have just said, 'What a nice gift' and left it at that."

"I'm not going to lie to you, Gina. There is too much at stake here."

"Listen I don't want to spoil this day either. It was beautiful and thanks for all you did. But I'm exhausted and going to bed."

"I'm only protecting you because I love you so much. I want you to keep getting better. I'm not going to let you go back to that dark place."

"I know. But some of this I have to process in my own way."

Anna didn't react. She just gave her a hug and walked out the door and drove to Christian's. She had to go there first before confronting her mother.

~

Anna had just finished her story and Christian finally weighed in.

"I don't know, Anna. Maybe Gina is right. Maybe

this is Mom's olive branch."

She jumped up from her chair at the kitchen table. "Are you kidding me? The woman went to a lawyer. Twice! Then she goes home and forgets about it and purchases a gift and it's all better."

She paused before continuing, trying to choose her words wisely as she knew Christian would get upset.

"Before you get all soft on Mom, I haven't told you the worst part of the story. Gina believes what Mom has been telling her. She thinks she is to blame for the accident."

"No, she doesn't."

"She told me, Christian. She actually said, 'Maybe Helena is finally going to forgive me.' Forgive her!"

Christian put his face in his hands.

"We were probably stupid to think Gina didn't blame herself. And how would we know. We weren't here for her. We never asked her."

"Christian, we are past that now. Let's not go back there. Gina has forgiven us."

"This is a mess, Anna. How are we supposed to know what Mom is thinking? How do we know it's not genuine? You are the one that has been praying not me. Maybe this is God answering your prayers. Maybe Mom is sorry and maybe Gina is ready to put down the guilt. Who are we not to believe it?"

"I hate it when you might be right."

"Might?"

"Yes, might, I'm not being that stupid. We have to protect her. I mean it."

"I know, sis. We will."

~

Two days after the shower Gina's phone rang and

she knew it was her mother—again. She was avoiding her calls. She figured she knew it was Helena who dropped the present and was just looking for the latest details. Though Gina had to admit she was curious to know if the two women exchanged words. She hit answer and took a deep breath.

"Hey, Mom," she tried to say easily.

"Gina, I was getting worried about you."

"Mom, sometimes I need space. And I know why you were calling and really I don't want to talk about it."

"What was in the box?"

"Gee, Mom thanks for listening."

"Come on, Gina."

"It was a frame with a photo of me, Alex and Teresa and something inscribed for the baby."

Silence.

"Mom. Say something."

"She's up to something, you know that right?"

"Maybe."

"Maybe?"

"I don't know, Mom. I don't have the energy to think about all this. It's exhausting. But now it's my turn. Did you all talk?"

"Barely. I just told her to leave before anyone saw her as I didn't want her spoiling your day. Did she?"

"Not really."

"A little?"

"Yeah, but mainly it messed up things between me and Anna. I feel bad about it but haven't reached out to her."

"You should, Gina. I can tell that girl cares about you and she is putting you first and not her mother. We all are just trying to protect you."

"I know. Thanks, Mom."

"Always."

She ended the call and figured she may as well get the next one over with. But she didn't have the energy to talk so she sent a simple text to Anna.

"I'm sorry."

"Me too."

"Girls night this week?"

"Absolutely."

Gina was on a roll so figured she would keep up the streak. She pulled up Helena's number. "Thank you for the beautiful frame."

"Welcome," was the only response.

With that kind of answer Gina wondered why Helena even sent it in the first place.

Chapter 16

Gina lay on the table with her legs in the stirrups while the visiting doctor performed the exam. Her regular OB was called out on an emergency and Gina had never seen this one before. His bedside manor left a lot to be desired.

"Still no dilation, but that's normal for two weeks out. Are you ready?"

"Ready?"

"You know bag packed. Plans for when you go into labor. But you have been through this before you will be fine. Is your daughter excited?"

He said all that while looking at the chart which clearly didn't say her daughter was dead. Gina glanced at the nurse--her favorite who knew her whole history, and she could see the blood drain from her face as she turned a pale white.

"She's dead and so is my husband."

He looked at the nurse. Looked at Gina and said, "Well you are doing fine," and walked out the door.

Nobody moved.

"Gina …"

"Don't. It's fine. In fact these are the things I need to get used to. I need to get a thick skin. How would he have known?"

"He's a jerk."

The corners of Gina's mouth turned up only slightly. "Thanks for saying that."

"Really, nobody likes him. But even I can't believe he did that."

"It's fine," she said, willing her tears back in her eyelids. "I just want to get dressed and go home."

"Sure," she said not knowing what else to do or say, so she just patted her on the shoulder and left the room.

The door had barely shut when the tears came like a waterfall. She tried to shut her mouth so she wouldn't be doing the convulsing crying. How she was going to get herself out of this room?

She pulled on her clothes, wiped her eyes as best she could and ran out the door not making eye contact with anyone. She heard the woman at the desk try to stop her to make her appointment for the following week but she just yelled out that she would call.

She pulled up to Christian's and saw a car outside, but wasn't sure whose, so she drove the five extra minutes to Anna's but there was a car there also. She texted Elizabeth. "Really need to talk," but there was no answer.

She punched in Grace's number. "Help," was all she could manage.

"Be there in 15 minutes."

Gina pulled in her driveway only five minutes before Grace appeared at the door armed with junk food.

"What did you bring?"

"What do you need?"

"My husband," and she fell into Grace's arms and wept another river of tears she didn't know she had.

When she finally stopped crying, Grace opened the bags of chips, but Gina noticed she brought along a few semi healthy things like dried mangoes, Gina's favorite. She laughed loudly when she saw her pull out a jar of pickles.

"I don't know what people crave these days," said Grace. "Want to talk about it?"

Gina relayed what happened at the doctor and Grace vowed to call the office the next morning and ream them out.

"Please don't. It's not even that. It's that a simple comment can make me fall apart. I am so scared, Grace. Yes I know I have friends and family but they aren't with me every minute. And I miss him. I just miss him so much. And my baby. I miss her too."

"I know," she said, pulling her in as she would her own daughter. "But it wasn't a simple comment, Gina. It was awful. Anyone would react like you are."

"How do I deal with it?"

"Day by day. Eventually you toughen up. Sadly, the more you hear it the less it bothers you."

"It sounds like you are speaking from experience."

"I have dealt with people like that doctor ten-fold. It was so hard, and it makes me angry that you are going through this also. I pray for you every day and will continue to do so."

"Thank you, Grace. I'm sorry I was mean to you when I first came to group."

"I know. We were all like that, Gina. Now we can see the forest through the trees but you are still lost in the brush. But you will get through it. Promise to call me any time."

~

"I can't believe you are one week away from your due date," said Anna as she sat on Gina's couch while scrolling through the guide looking for a good flick to watch.

"When is your next doctor appointment?" Elizabeth asked, while grabbing a barbecue chip from the bag.

"Tomorrow."

"Do you feel different?"

Gina laughed. "Not really. Just scared."

They both looked at her afraid to ask more but wanting to be there for her.

"I know you guys are reluctant to ask me stuff—and that's my fault—but I really want to talk about it."

"We are here for you," said Anna. "Tell us what you are afraid of."

"Everything. That all these emotions are going to come up during delivery—and after—I'm afraid I am going to sink into a depression like before that I won't be able to get out of—and this time I have to."

"Your doctor knows about all this, right?" asked Elizabeth. "She can get whatever help you need, right?"

"Yeah, and I was going to ask you guys. Can you watch Alex on Monday nights so I can still go to my grief group? I think that is going to be even more important to me after the baby comes to help me through all this."

"Of course," Anna said. "We will be fighting over who gets to watch him."

"You guys are the best. Let's find a good comedy to watch."

Gina seemed to enjoy it but for the next hour and a half all Elizabeth and Anna could think about was whether or not their friend was going to be okay.

~

Christian couldn't concentrate at work that Friday. He kept thinking about what Anna had told him about Gina, and he wondered why she hadn't called him this week or returned any of his texts so he shot off a message to her. "Miss you. Stopping by your house tonight after work."

~

"Hey, Gina. Long time no see."

She looked at Christian standing at her door, still seeing Alex, and wondering if that would ever go away.

"I saw you last week. And I stopped by your house the other day but there was a car there, so I just went home."

"That was my friend from work who stopped by for a few beers. You should have come in."

"No, really I shouldn't have. I was in a bad place."

"I'm sorry. I wish I knew."

"Christian, you can't be there for me every time I am having a tough time."

"But I want to be. And Alex would want me to."

"No, he would want you to find a woman to settle down with and not worry about me."

"I know for a fact he would want me to worry about you."

She shot him a curious glance. "Is that why you check up on me? As a duty to your dead brother?"

"Gina!"

"I'm sorry I said it that way but I don't need your pity, Christian."

"What the heck, Gina. I know you don't. I told you I want to be here. We used to be best friends—the three of us. You know that. I don't know why you are acting like this."

"The three of us. You don't have to keep doing that now that he is gone if you don't want to."

He reached his hand across the table. "Stop. I want to be here. You know that. And you like hanging out with me too. You and I were friends too. We had so much fun together, and we talked about everything."

"I just don't want to be dependent on anyone like that again," she said fighting back tears.

"But you have to be. That's what life is. It throws you heartache and you lean on others. And when life throws them heartache, they lean on you. And when two friends lose the same person—one their husband and daughter and the other their sibling and niece—they rely on each other."

And then he reached over and wiped away her tears.

~

The contractions woke her up that night. She threw the cover off and grabbed her phone from the bedside table and called Elizabeth.

"Gina, are you okay?"

"It's time."

"Be there in ten minutes."

While waiting she texted Anna and Christian to tell them she was on her way to the hospital. Then she texted her mother.

~

When Elizabeth picked her up Gina cried the whole

way. She just couldn't stop. She knew Elizabeth was afraid she was going to have a nervous breakdown right there while in labor but she couldn't control it.

"Gina. It's going to be okay. You have to believe that. You are strong and you need to remember that and get yourself together so you can deliver a healthy baby."

They pulled up then and two EMTs came over to help. Elizabeth panicked. She couldn't just hand Gina off in this state while she went to park the car. Right then she saw Christian and Anna drive up and Anna jumped out to talk to Elizabeth. She took one look at Gina and gave Elizabeth a worried look.

"Thank goodness you are here. Do me a favor and take Gina to go get checked in while Christian and I go park the cars."

"Okay," she said tentatively all while staring at Gina's tear stained face, which now looked a little comatose.

"Yes, she is freaking out. So, make sure you tell the nurses her situation, so they are aware."

"Elizabeth, do you think she can do this?"

"Does she have a choice? And yes, she can. She is strong, and we just have to remind her of that."

Anna walked over to the passenger side to help Gina into the wheelchair the EMTs had waiting for her.

Elizabeth parked the car but before heading back to the hospital she texted Grace. "We need you. Gina is in labor and a wreck. You will know what to do. And pray!"

"Come on, Elizabeth. We have to get up there," said Christian.

"I know. Calm down. Give me a minute."

"Elizabeth, what's wrong?"

"Christian, you didn't see her. I'm really worried about her."

"Okay, well standing here isn't doing her any good."

"Listen, Christian, I need to pray before I go up there."

"Now? Here?"

"Yes, right here."

"Alright," and he grabbed her hand and bowed his head while Elizabeth asked God to take over in this situation and be with Gina through this difficult time.

~

"Wait here," said Elizabeth, when they finally found Gina's hospital room. "Let me make sure she is decent."

"Good idea," then he stood uncomfortably outside the door. She appeared in less than a minute motioning him inside.

"Hey, Gina," said Christian as he walked over and kissed her on the cheek. She gave him a half-hearted smile and looked back at Anna whose face revealed nothing but worry.

Dr. Bellini came in then, took a look at all three of them and said one person could stay.

"Elizabeth is my partner in this," as she reached out her hand to her.

"Great." I will call you two back when I am done examining her.

Anna and Christian walked out the door their faces lined with so much worry.

"Well, Gina it looks like you are four centimeters dilated. Now is the time if you want some pain medication."

Elizabeth prayed to herself, "Please say yes, please say yes."

"Sure," was all Gina said, as she wriggled in the bed bracing herself through another contraction.

"Okay, great I'll call for the anesthesiologist. I will be back in an hour or so to check on you."

Again, Gina was silent.

"Hey, I will be right back," said Elizabeth. "But I'll send Anna and Christian in to keep you company."

She walked outside and told the two siblings to go with Gina while she grabbed the doctor.

"Dr. Bellini, wait," yelled Elizabeth as she followed her down the hallway.

"I wanted to talk to you for a minute. I'm really worried about her."

"I know. I am too," which did nothing to assuage Elizabeth's fears.

"Well, what can we do to help?"

"You just need to be there for her. It's all in her chart. Everyone working with her today knows of her status. They know she is emotionally fragile. They know what she has been through and know the signs of what to look for."

"The signs?"

"Of a nervous breakdown."

"Oh God."

"I'm not saying that it's going to happen, Elizabeth, but you've seen her. This is a lot. I can only imagine she has been suppressing a lot of her feelings ever since the deaths. And now she is delivering a baby and all those emotions are coming out. It's totally normal. She will get through it and everyone is keeping a close eye on her. The best thing you can do is just go be with your friend. Tell her she is strong because she is. Remind her of what she has gotten through so far."

"Okay, but let's say she doesn't have a full on breakdown which I'm hoping she doesn't. Obviously, she is battling depression and a lot of healthy women have postpartum depression let alone someone who has lost her husband and daughter less than a year ago. How will we help her with that?"

"There is medicine we can give her to help her and I know she will need that. In fact, I have already written a prescription in her chart. But it's not a cure all. I suggest you and your friends, and her family, try to make sure she is with someone for a while until you can gauge how she is doing."

"Yeah, we can do that."

"Don't worry, Elizabeth. We are talking about the bad side but there could be a great outcome from this. The baby could really help her heal. And even if you don't see that happening from the beginning doesn't mean it won't. Hang in there and continue to support her through all these phases she will go through."

"Thank you."

"You're welcome. And one more thing. Make sure she is surrounded by those who love her. Now is not the time for drama."

"Wait, what has Gina told you?"

"She hasn't told me anything. But every family has drama. And the people who bring it need to stay away. She has enough going on right now and none of that will help her move forward especially in the beginning when she is extremely fragile."

The doctor walked away, and Anna knew her last

request would be the hardest of all.

~

Two hours later Dr. Bellini examined Gina and reported she was at ten centimeters, and it was time to push.

"Okay, that's our cue," said Christian, as he walked over and took Gina's hand. "Anna and I will be waiting outside. You got this."

"Thanks."

"Love you," said Anna as she walked out the door.

"Alright, Gina this is it," said Dr. Bellini. "I know you are tired and want to quit but you are strong. You have to give this everything you got. And you have an amazing friend to help you through."

All Gina could think about was the last time she was here at this hospital. The images flooded her. Alex by her side, pushing back her hair. Telling her how much he loved her. Feeding her ice chips. Kissing her on the cheek.

"Gina. Do you hear me? It's time."

"I can't."

"Yes, you can," said Elizabeth. "Where did you go just then? Were you thinking about Alex?"

"The images just came flooding back. Of being here when Teresa was born. I feel paralyzed."

Elizabeth looked at Dr. Bellini, her eyes full of fear.

"Gina, you have to push. If you don't, I have to prep you for a C section right now and I don't think that is the best option for you. I know you can do this but you have to believe it. Can you do this?"

Then she saw Alex. He was standing next to her bed telling her she could and that he would be here with her.

"I can."

~

"He's here," said Elizabeth smiling brightly as she greeted Christian, Anna, and now Grace, in the waiting room."

"How is she?" asked Christian.

"She seems okay. It was rough," then Elizabeth broke down in tears, while Christian and Anna stood in shock.

"Listen you two go in and see your sister-in-law," said Grace. "I'll stay here with Elizabeth for a bit. She has been through a lot too."

They just stared.

"Go."

"Come here, honey," said Grace, as she led her to an area with a few chairs and gestured for her to sit down. "Let it all out."

"I feel bad. Why am I crying? I should be strong. But I am so worried about her, Grace. You didn't see her."

"I know. But we hurt when others do. You need to just let this out before you go back in there. You have been up all night. You are exhausted and worried. It's going to be okay."

She lay her head on Grace's shoulder and fell asleep.

~

Christian and Anna walked in the room to see Gina looking drained and holding her baby boy on her chest. "Hey, Gina," said Christian. "You did it."

"Yeah, I did. And look at your precious nephew."

"He is gorgeous," said Anna who had to hold back tears when she saw how much he looked like Alex.

"He's gonna be a looker, just like his dad," said

Christian. "I'm sorry. Should I not have said that?"

"It's okay, Christian. It's all I can think about. Look how much he resembles him."

"It's amazing," said Anna. "I want to hold him but he looks so peaceful sleeping so I will get my chance later."

"Do you want us to leave you so you can get some rest?"

"I am exhausted. But you can stay."

"We can hang out and let you sleep if you want. That way we are here if he starts to stir and you can continue to get some rest," said Christian.

"You guys are awesome. What would I do without you?"

About a minute later she was breathing heavily finally letting sleep take over.

Anna whispered to Christian. "Want to flip for who calls home?"

Christian laughed. "I got it sis. You stay here while I go call Dad."

~

"Hey, Christian what's up?"

"Well, I just wanted to tell you that Anna and I won't be able to come for Sunday dinner today. We are at the hospital with your new grandson."

"That's great news. Did everything go okay?" and Christian could hear the concern in his voice as he must have been mentally checking off all the things that could have gone wrong.

"Everything is great, Dad."

"I'll get dressed and come to the hospital. Do you think Gina would be okay with that?"

"She had a pretty rough 24 hours. Do you think you

could come tomorrow?"

"Of course."

"Dad. He looks exactly like Alex."

John hung up the phone to find Helena standing behind him.

"What's wrong, John?"

"Nothing," he said, while wiping a stray tear. "It's good news. Gina had the baby. We have a grandson."

"Well let's go."

"Not today. And I am surprised you think you should even go at all. I told Christian I would come tomorrow after Gina is able to get some rest."

"I don't care about, Gina. We are going to see our grandson."

"Did you hear what you just said, Helena? You don't care about Gina. You are not going there. Oh, and the kids won't be over for dinner today," then he turned and walked upstairs.

About 30 minutes later, John heard the door shut. He ran outside and saw his wife get into a car, with the Uber logo on the back.

He texted Anna and Christian. "Your mother just got in an Uber. I'm so sorry. Look out for her and warn Gina. I'm on my way."

They both saw the text at the same time. "What is wrong with our mother?" said Christian. "I'm going to go stand guard outside but we both know even I can't keep her out. All we can do right now is pray."

Christian walked out of the room and told Grace and Elizabeth what happened. Elizabeth, who had finally stopped crying, started again and Grace rubbed her back and once again told her it was going to be okay.

"Listen guys," said Grace. "Yes, it would have been better if this happened in a day or two. But it was inevitable so it's better we get it over with and have everyone here to protect her. It would have been worse if Gina had to endure this alone unexpectedly."

"You are right," said Elizabeth. "You know, we have always said to each other how lucky Gina is to have you, but all of us are blessed to have found you."

And then it was Grace's turn to cry.

"How did I get so lucky to have found another family in all you kids?"

They all hugged then walked back in the room to warn Gina, who was awake now as Alex had stirred.

"Hey, Gina, look at this precious baby boy of yours," said Grace as she bent down to kiss Gina on the cheek.

"Isn't he amazing?" said Gina.

"Did you get enough sleep?" asked Christian.

"Enough. No. But yes, I feel a little better. I mean look at this guy. How can I not?"

Alex started to cry, and Gina pulled him close and made calming sounds in his ear.

"I think it's time for him to eat. Can someone hand me that bottle?"

"Of course," said Christian, handing it over. "Anna and I were going to step out anyway, but first she has to tell you something. I will be right outside."

Gina's face fell. "Please Anna. Please tell me it's not happening already? Your mother is not on her way here?"

"She is. Dad tried to stop her but she got in an Uber without him knowing. Apparently, that's her thing now."

"I can't. I can't," and the three women could tell she was about to get hysterical again.

"Listen, Gina. We got this," said Grace. "I don't know that we can stop her coming in here and maybe we just want to get it over with. But believe me when I say we have your back."

"Thank you. Grace, can you please pray?"

"Already done, sweetheart. I've been flooding heaven with prayer since I heard your mother-in-law was on her way."

"I'm going to wait outside with my brother. You feed this precious baby of yours and I will see you soon. I'm going to go flood heaven with some more prayers myself. The more the better, right?"

Then Grace and Elizabeth sat with Gina while she fed Alex, and no one said a word while they waited for the storm that was Helena Andros to descend on the hospital.

~

Anna and Christian saw her coming and met her at the elevator before she could ask the nurse for Gina's room number.

"Don't bother telling me I shouldn't be here."

"I never knew how selfish you were until now," said Anna.

"Selfish?"

"Yes, selfish. This isn't about you."

"That's my grandson in there."

"Yes, and he is with his mother," Anna continued. "A woman you shunned from the family and have treated horribly. You should have known your actions would have consequences when it came to him. You think she is just going to welcome you with open arms?

Actually, it's Gina we are talking about. She probably would."

"Mom, all we are saying is you can't continue to treat Gina horribly and still expect to have a relationship with your grandson," said Christian. "It doesn't work like that."

The elevator dinged and John walked off the elevator all red in the face from undoubtedly running to catch Helena before she wreaked havoc.

"Hey Dad," said Anna.

"Hey, so since I am here do I get to go see my grandson," he said never even looking in Helena's direction.

"Sure, let's go," and Helena started to follow.

Anna pulled her arm. "Mom, best behavior."

She ignored her and followed Christian down the hallway.

John walked in first and went straight to Gina who was holding Alex on her chest. "Hey Gina. Congratulations. You look amazing."

Gina smiled, remembering that John always doled out compliments, always making her feel special. Like father like son.

"Meet your grandson. Do you want to hold him?"

"I would love to," then she tenderly handed Alex off to his grandfather.

"He looks just like him."

"I know," was all she could say.

Helena had been standing in the doorway watching it all and wondering who the older woman in the chair was. She walked in and said, "Hello, Gina," in a voice she would have used to greet someone she was just meeting for the first time, and barely looked her way.

Then she went straight for Alex and scooped him right out of John's arms. "Look at my precious grandson. Oh you look just like your father."

She continued this way for minutes, not acknowledging anyone else in the room. It was Grace who finally broke the silence.

"So that's how it's going to be huh," said Grace, as her eyes honed in on Helena.

"Excuse me?"

"I can't believe you come in here and barely say hello to your daughter-in-law, and then you just take over with the baby. You can't treat her like that. She is his mother. She deserves respect."

"She deserves nothing. And who are you?"

"Oh, I apologize. I'm Grace. I'm one of the people, along with your two children, who has been here for Gina while you were off visiting lawyers."

Helena's olive skin faded to pure white. For once Helena was speechless. No one had ever spoken to her like that.

"You need to leave. You are welcome back anytime when you are ready to treat her with respect."

Helena handed the baby to Christian who had been standing closest to her and left the room. John followed and mouthed an "I'm sorry" to Gina as he left.

"So that's Helena?" said Grace, and Gina couldn't help but smile and thank God for bringing this feisty woman into her life.

~

Helena and John were almost home, and his wife still hadn't said a word and he wasn't about to engage her. There was nothing to say. Grace had said it all, and John was so happy she did. No one in the family had the guts to speak up to Helena. They needed an outsider to come in and plainly point out Helena's behavior. John just hoped that some of it sunk in. But knowing his wife, there was little chance of that happening.

They walked in the house in silence when John heard his phone vibrate. It was a text from Christian. "How bad is it?" "Nothing but silence," he texted back.

"Anna and I decided we aren't going to reach out to her. We think it's good what Grace said. Mom is the one who has to figure this out. We are sick of being in the middle of it."

"I agree. And tell Grace I said thanks."

Christian looked at that last part and smiled, then looked up from his phone.

"So," said Grace. "Was that your Dad? Does he hate me?"

"He actually wants me to thank you."

"I do too," said Anna. "None of us have had the guts to stand up to her like that," then she looked at Gina.

"Will you forgive us?"

"Forgive you? For what? Who has been here with me through all this? You two. So you didn't stand up to your mother. You shouldn't have to. She's your mother. And I didn't do it either. I know I should have, and next time I just hope I have the strength. Because we all know there is going to be a next time. Helena doesn't give up."

Gina went on. "But can we just all take a second and admit that what Grace did was amazing."

And for the second time that day Grace had to reach for a tissue. It was Elizabeth who lightened the mood, as she could tell Grace didn't like the attention. "Okay, who wants to be on duty tonight?"

Before she could continue, Christian's hand shot up and everyone laughed.

"No argument here, Bro. I'm beat."

"Me too," said Elizabeth.

Before Grace left she turned back toward Gina. "When do your Mom and Dad get here?"

"Tomorrow."

"Okay maybe I will give you some space the next few days."

"Sure, but stay by your phone. If I send you an SOS that means my Mom is hovering and you have to come rescue me."

Grace laughed and said she would check in with her in a day or so.

And then it was just Christian and Gina.

"Christian, you don't have to stay. I know you guys are worried but I'm in a hospital for goodness sake. If I need someone there are plenty of people around."

"Who said I stayed for you? I'm here to hang out with this guy," as he stroked Alex's cheek while he lay sleeping in the hospital bassinet.

"Well, thank you. But can I tell you something?"

"Anything."

"I'm worried about eventually being alone. I have all these people now but what happens when my parents come and go, when everyone has to go back to work and it's just me and him. Promise to not tell anyone, Christian. But I'm scared."

"I'm glad you are being honest, Gina. I think that is half the battle here—asking for help. You are right. We won't be around every minute—but you have to know that when you need us—we are here—no matter what."

"Thanks, Chris."

"Welcome, G."

Then they both sat back in silence wondering how long it had been since they had used those nicknames for each other. Definitely before the accident--before everything changed.

"As much as I love talking to you, I have been around long enough to hear that old adage, sleep when the baby sleeps. So you get some rest and I will be here when you need me."

"Thank you. I will," and then she was out.

~

Gina didn't know what time it was when she woke up and glimpsed Christian holding the baby, swaying him from side to side and singing ever so quietly in his ear a song that Alex had always sang. She pretended she was still sleeping and let the silent tears fall. She would give anything to have Alex with her right now. For it to be how it was when Teresa was born. And then the tears came harder and she couldn't control her sobs.

"Gina, what's wrong?" as he came over with Alex still in his arms.

"It's too much."

"What's too much?"

"The memories, Christian. I can't make them stop."

And at that moment Sal and Maria Galliano walked in the room.

"What's wrong, Gina? Christian what's wrong with her?"

"Calm down, Maria," her father said as he came over and kissed on her on the cheek. "How is my baby girl?"

"I'll be okay, Dad. I'm just overwhelmed by

memories right now. I'll get myself back together."

"You don't have to do that Gina. Let it out. It's not good to keep everything inside. Don't let your mother freak you out. It's okay to cry."

Maria glared at Sal. "Yes, I'm sorry, Gina. You know how I get."

"No, not you?"

Maria laughed then finally turned toward Christian who was holding Alex. She put her hands up to her face. "Gina, he looks …"

"I know. Isn't it crazy?"

"It really is," said Sal. "What a beautiful little boy."

"Do you want to hold him grandpa?" asked Christian.

"Yes!" and Christian carefully handed him off then walked over to Gina and whispered in her ear. "Enjoy your family. But text me if you need backup."

She smiled, and Maria saw it all, wondering what to make of how close those two were becoming again.

~

Dr. Bellini walked in while Gina was resting in the bed and her parents were sitting on the couch oohing and ahhing over Alex.

"Hey, Gina, how are you feeling today?"

"Okay."

"Well, you can go home today but I wanted to talk to you about a few things before I release you."

Her parents looked at Dr. Bellini and took the cue. "We will go grab a cup of coffee," then her father passed Alex back to Gina.

"Sounds good, Dad. Take your time."

"That was your parents I take it."

"Yup. They will be staying with me for at least two

weeks. They won't tell me when they are leaving, and I know it's because they won't go until they know I am doing okay."

"And are you?"

"I think so. I love this baby, but there are so many memories. And when they hit me out of nowhere, they literally knock me over."

"And what do you do when that happens?"

"Well so far someone has always been here to take care of the baby while I process it all."

"It seems like you have a great support system."

"I do. I have my four dear friends all close by who I know will be here for me day or night."

"You have to take advantage of that, you know that right?

"I do."

"I mean it. You won't always need them. But when you do, you need to call them and lean on them. That's the only way this is going work."

"I know. Really I do."

"Good. So while you have been here we have been giving you Zoloft and I want to keep that up for a while. You have enough going on Gina and that will help you in these first few months. Especially since we know you went through postpartum depression last time."

"Yes, I agree."

"Do you feel well enough to head home? Be honest with me."

"I do."

"Alright then let me go put in your paperwork. And I will see you in my office in a week."

"Sounds great."

Then she left the room hoping to find Gina's parents. She needed to give them a few instructions as well.

"Sal? Maria?" said Dr. Bellini as she saw them rounding the corner with their coffee cups.

"Hi. Oh, is Gina waiting for us? We better get in there."

"Actually, she and the baby are resting. And I wanted to talk to you both."

"Is she going to be okay?" asked Maria.

"Yes, she will. But it's a fine line to walk around her and I just wanted to give you some tips," to which Maria seemed to bristle.

"There is no perfect way to act. She will have good days and bad. And you have to gauge those and react as they come. You need to look for signs of depression, yet not hover. Like I said it's hard. But when she needs space you need to give it to her, while at the same time checking in to make sure she is still okay."

"How are we supposed to make sense of that?" asked Maria.

"It's easy, Maria," said her husband. "You have to read the signs. You can't just plow ahead and smother her."

"He's right," said Dr. Bellini. "The way others act around her will make a huge difference in her recovery."

"Recovery? asked Maria with surprise.

"Yes, recovery. Don't you agree she is still putting herself back together after her losses?"

"Well, yes but …"

"But nothing, you have to give her all the time she needs."

"What makes you an expert?" Maria shot back.

"I work with expecting mothers every single day. From when they get pregnant to after the delivery and all the emotions in between." Before she could defend herself more, Sal cut her off knowing it wasn't necessary.

"Yes, we know you have expertise here and we are going to listen." Then Sal wondered if his wife didn't have a stubborn streak as strong as Helena's.

Dr. Bellini left, none of her worries about her patient having subsided. In fact, she was now more concerned than before. Maybe the brother-in-law was the one she should have talked to. Gina and he certainly seemed to have an amazing bond. Maybe he would be the best one to help her through this.

~

Gina hadn't been home from the hospital an hour and her mother was already asking a million questions. What should I make when here? What cleaning do you want me to do? The list went on.

"Mom, I won't be doing any of those things so knock yourself out. I won't complain about any of it. But I don't want to make any decisions, okay?"

"You're right. You just take care of the baby and when you need to sleep, I will take care of him for you."

"Thanks, Mom. That's really all I want. I just want to get used to all this and it will be nice to have some help."

"That's what we are here for. And, of course we hope to get tons of time cuddling with this little one," she said as he nuzzled Alex's cheek while he lay asleep in Gina's lap.

"What do you want to do about tonight?" asked her mother.

"Tonight?"

"Yes. When the baby gets up do you want me to wake up for at least one of those so you can sleep?"

What was wrong with her? She hadn't even thought that far ahead. At the hospital she had all these people around to help.

"I don't know, Mom. Let's just see how it goes. If I need you, I will come get you." Silently, she was determined not to have to rely on her mother.

~

The family was all relaxing lazily on the living room couches, passing the baby to one another, when Alex had finally fallen asleep around 11 p.m.

"Well guys, I'm going to head up with Alex and hopefully get a few hours in. Have a good night."

"You too, sweetheart."

Three hours later, Gina awoke to his cries from the bassinet that sat next to her bed. She reached over hoping rocking it would allow him to fall back asleep but no such luck. She left him there then hurried downstairs to make a bottle without waking her parents.

She came back upstairs, picked him up and walked into his room without even thinking and sat down on the rocker. And the images came fast. Gina rocking Teresa on her first night home from the hospital. Alex coming over without saying a word, taking his little girl from her arms, and guiding Gina back to bed so she could get some rest. That image would not be repeated tonight, and her heart ached.

Alex finished his bottle and Gina lifted him over her shoulder to burp him, hoping to quickly get out of this room and away from these memories. He wriggled and whined and would not rock back to sleep no matter what she did.

"Why are you making this so hard for me?" she said to him, right before Maria was about to enter the room. She quickly tiptoed back before Gina would know she was there.

"I love you. I do. But I want your Dad back. I want your sister. Why are you here and not them? I want all of us together as a family."

Maria had to suck in her breath so Gina wouldn't hear her crying in the hallway. She tiptoed back to where she had come and wondered if her daughter was going to be okay ever again.

~

At seven the next morning, Maria heard the baby crying, and went straight to Gina's room. "Honey, I know you couldn't have slept much last night. Can I take him from you so you can sleep for a few hours?"

"Yes, thank you. I don't know what I would do without you."

She walked downstairs and handed the baby to Sal who was sitting with a cup of coffee while she made the bottle. And she told him what she heard the night before. He put down his mug and held his head. "Maria? Is our little girl going to be okay?"

"We have to pray she will be, Sal. She is tired and lonely."

"But we're here," then he stopped. "You are right. The two people she wants the most are gone."

~

Gina didn't come downstairs for four hours, but when she did, she enveloped her mother in an embrace.

"Thank you so much for letting me rest. That was so much harder than I remember. I'm exhausted."

"You are welcome, honey. I will have to keep doing that until the baby gets into more of a routine and sleeps for longer periods at a time."

She looked over at Alex sleeping in his swing and smiled. "Has he been good?"

"The best," said Sal easily.

"Mom, can you make me pancakes?" Maria lit up instantly and set off to work.

"Why don't you go shower quick while the baby is sleeping, and I am cooking."

"Good idea. I better get it when I can right?

"Yeah, and you stink." She swatted her father playfully at his comment then left the room.

Chapter 17

A week later, Gina set off to the one-week follow-up doctor's appointment with Alex in tow.

"Are you sure you don't want to leave Alex here?"

"No," Gina said, even though her heart was beating heavily in her chest. "I need to get used to going out with him before you all leave me. And Dr. Bellini would kill me. She told me to bring him to the appointment."

Her mother kissed her on the cheek, admiring her daughter's tenacity and began to worry, which she would do until Gina walked back in the door.

Gina found herself calming down. The trip was uneventful, they were now seated in the waiting room and Alex was fast asleep. She did get sad when she saw all the families here for their appointments, but she had to get used to that. It was just her and Alex now. She was doing pretty well, considering.

"Gina?" She turned to see an old friend, who was lovely, with her husband, who was anything but. Alex and Gina always used to wonder how those two got together.

They both looked down at her baby in silence. Thirty seconds must have passed—time enough for Ellen to do the math in her head. Her husband wasn't as smart though. "A baby? Wow you didn't let much time pass before you moved on?"

"Dave," Ellen snapped, horrified, which was evident by the beet color of her face.

"I'm sorry, Gina. I am so sorry."

Gina vaguely remembered hearing Alex cry then from there it went blank. From how it was relayed to her after, the nurse called out Ellen's name and she went back for her appointment not knowing what else to do but leave Gina there.

Alex started crying harder and Gina heard none of it. Another one of the nurse's came out, one Gina knew and liked, and led her back to one of the patient rooms while another nurse followed with the baby. They allowed her to rest on the exam table while one of the nurses stayed with her trying to calm her down and find out what happened, all while constantly monitoring her heart rate and blood pressure. When she opened her eyes and didn't see Alex she panicked. "Where's my baby?"

"It's okay Gina," said Dr. Bellini. "Here he is. All the nurses have loved having him here. You may have found yourself some babysitters."

She reached over to take him but Dr. Bellini said she needed to get a little stronger first and the nurse handed her a glass of ice water.

"Gina, what happened?" Dr. Bellini asked.

"I ran into a friend of mine and her jerk of a

husband who said, and I quote: You didn't waste any time getting pregnant."

"Oh Gina, I am so sorry. Wait, was it Ellen's husband?"

"Yes."

"I never liked that guy. How those two got together I will never know."

"Yup."

"Well, look at it this way. Your next venture out of the house can't be worse than this one."

Gina laughed. "One can hope."

Your blood pressure and heart rate is still really elevated. I don't want you driving home. Can you call someone to get you?"

She texted Anna and Christian.

~

The ugliness of the afternoon behind them, Anna and Christian sat at the table now with Gina and her parents enjoying an amazing Italian meal made by Maria. Christian was still threatening to track Dave down and make him pay for what he did to Gina. It was very sweet but Gina just wanted to forget it.

"Why don't you kids go visit and your father and I will clean up in here."

"Kids?" answered Christian playfully.

"Sorry, why don't you adults go visit."

"I'll stay here with you and help," said Anna, knowing Christian wanted to talk to Gina, and she wouldn't mind some time picking Maria's brain about how her friend was doing.

Alex started crying then, and Gina scooped him up and said she was taking him upstairs to change him, while Christian followed behind. He was silent the whole time Gina went about the nighttime routine with the baby. She couldn't take it anymore.

"Just say it, Christian."

"I want to kill that guy."

"The macho thing is cute and all but you really need to get over it."

Did she just use the word cute? Now she threw him off his game and he didn't know what to say.

"How am I supposed to get over it? How am I supposed to know you aren't going to fall apart again the next time someone says something like that to you. Because you know it's going to happen again."

So that's how he saw her. Someone who would fall apart at a moment's notice.

"I thought I was safe to tell you that, Chris. But now I know you can't handle it. I thought you were someone I could go to when I had a rough day. And today was a really awful day. And yes, I fell apart. I thought I could tell you when that happened."

"You can, Gina," but she wouldn't allow him to continue.

"I need you to listen, to console me, but not go beat up everyone who says something wrong. Because you are right--it will happen again and all I need is for you to be there for me. That's it."

"Gina."

She stopped him before he could continue. "Listen, I'm tired. Thanks for coming to get me today, really."

"Gina. I'm sorry. Please don't make me leave. I have missed you. I just want to be with you."

Something in the way he said it had changed and she stood in shock.

"I'm sorry. You know what I mean."

She wasn't sure she did. Not knowing what else to do he walked over to Alex, kissed him on the cheek and told him he would see him again soon and left the room.

Anna came up a few minutes later carrying a glass of wine.

"Alright, what did my idiot brother do this time?"

"Nothing," Gina said while eying her wine glass.

Anna noticed right away and immediately scolded herself for being so stupid. She noticed Gina didn't have wine with dinner, as she usually would. Anna and Maria talked about the fact that it was probably a good thing since she relied on it a lot to get through the days in the months following the accident. Maybe they never should have had it at the table tonight.

"Sorry, maybe I shouldn't have brought this up here, nodding to her wine glass. I notice you didn't have any earlier. Does it bother you?"

"No, and I don't miss it. Am I a little afraid to drink some now in my emotional state, yes? So I'm staying away and I'm good with that. But I do have some emergency chocolate stashes all around the house."

"Yum. I'll have to go looking for those one day. So, want to tell me what my brother said?"

"Not really."

"You know he just cares about you right?

"I know."

"Do you think he's going to rip Dave's head off?"

"God only knows. I just hope those two don't run into each other in a dark alley."

Anna laughed. "Well, I better leave you to it. I'll text you and come by in a few days."

"Sounds good."

~

"Are you ready to admit it?" asked Anna while Christian drove her home.

"Admit what?"

"Don't."

She always could read his mind. He thought he was doing a good job hiding his emotions, but Anna always knew what was going on with him.

"Is it that obvious?"

"Only to those who really know you. Maria knows. I don't know if Gina does."

"She may after tonight."

"OMG spill. What happened up there?"

"Nothing I just may have said something about wanting to be with her. I don't know the way it came out just sounded different and she knew it. I only meant like hanging out with her."

"As more than friends?"

"I don't know, Anna. You know I always liked her, and that I always wanted what those two had. I mean yes, he's my brother and she just had his baby and he's not here and I am. I try to push these feelings down but I can't. I care about her."

"She cares about you too. And maybe one day Christian but it's too soon."

"Don't you think I know that? It just came out and really all I meant is that she is important to me and I didn't want to lose her just because I was going on about smashing Dave's skull in."

"But?"

"But I guess the way it came out made her nervous. I don't even know how it happened."

"It happened because you have always cared for

her. And you are worried about her and you know Alex would want you both to be happy."

~

"Did you think Christian was weird when he came back downstairs after talking to Gina?" Maria asked Sal, while rocking Alex. Gina was upstairs sleeping.

"Define weird," said Sal, while half listening, and watching the news on TV.

"I don't know. Different."

"Maybe," said Sal, though he hadn't really thought about it. Though now that he did, he said, "Yeah, maybe a little sad."

"You know he is sweet on her right?"

Sal turned toward Maria, ignoring the TV now. "Yes, I do know that. And I just wonder what Helena is going to do to our daughter when she figures it out."

"You're more intuitive than I thought, Sal Galliano."

"Gee, thanks." Now Maria got Sal thinking.

"You know, I get it though. Maybe he still just thinks of her as a friend but is just protective of her. I'm protective of her. Do you know what I wanted to do to Helena after I found out how she treated our daughter in the hospital? And John too. I mean get a backbone—stand up to your wife."

Maria stood up from her chair, walked over and kissed him on the cheek.

"What was that for?"

"You're just amazing that's all."

He smiled and went back to the news.

~

A week later Gina and her parents were sitting at the table eating Maria's homemade pancakes. No major disasters had occurred. Gina was getting some rest. Maria had stocked her fridge. No more inappropriate comments from the outside world had occurred (though Gina hadn't left the house but once to go to CVS), when Sal said the words Gina and her mother dreaded hearing.

"I think it's time for us to head home soon."

Gina put down her fork. She knew it was coming. They had been here two weeks now. Gina was doing okay all things considered. And she knew her practical father was going to announce that it was time Gina tried being on her own.

"Don't you think it's time you were on your own Gina—at least for a week or so? We can always come back whenever you need us for a long weekend or whatever you need."

She smiled slightly.

"What?"

"You're so predictable Dad. Mom and I had a bet you were going to say this today."

"Is that what you two do? Bet on me?"

"Pretty much," they both said in unison, then went back to their pancakes.

~

A few hours later, Maria sent a text to Anna, Christian and Elizabeth telling them they were headed home in two days and she would love if they would come for dinner the next night.

Christian replied first. "Are you sure she is ready for you to leave?"

Maria wasn't sure but she replied anyway. "Yes, but I need you all to be there for her when we are gone. It's the only way I won't worry."

"We got this," responded Anna.

"We will be there for her. She will be okay," said Elizabeth.

Christian didn't say a word. How could they know for sure?

~

Anna immediately called Elizabeth and when she picked up Anna launched right in. "Do you think it was weird that Maria didn't include Grace in that text?"

"Do I think it was weird that she didn't invite the woman she is jealous of, so she could make sure she will take care of her daughter? No, I don't think so at all."

"You think she is that jealous?"

"Come on, Anna. She was from the beginning and you should have seen her face when I told her the story of how Grace stood up for Gina in front of everyone. She tried to act pleased but you could tell she was jealous it wasn't she that was there for her daughter."

"You're right. So we won't throw it in her face but I'm going to text Grace and tell her Gina's parents are going to be gone in a few days and she is going to need us more than ever."

"One hundred percent agree," then they hung up.

~

They had just finished dinner which was full of loud banter, laughs and amazing food. In spite of it all, Gina was quieter than normal. Everyone looked at her and could see the tears welling in her eyelids. Her mother, who was seated next to her, reached over and rubbed her back, a familiar gesture that always made her feel better. She couldn't hold her tears any longer.

"I don't want you and Dad to go."

Elizabeth, Anna and Christian got up from the table. Christian picked up Alex who started to fuss while the two girls started clearing away dishes to the kitchen giving Gina and her parents some space.

"Gina, you are strong. You are going to be okay. It's not like we aren't coming back. I'm already planning our next trip to see you and my beautiful grandson. You need to prove to yourself you can do this."

Sal looked at his wife with love. After the accident she was always the one saying they had to stay and be there for her while Sal was saying she had to get through this on her own without them there every minute. He was shocked as he would have sworn that the next words out of her mouth were going to be that they could stay as long as she needed. He didn't give her enough credit, he supposed, and would apologize for that later.

"Gina, I can sit here and say you have this great support system, and you do," her mother went on. "But you also have this baby. Alex has already made you stronger. You are there for him, you are an amazing mother, and will continue to be. You got this. And when you fall down, which you will, your friends will be here to pick you up again."

"Your mother is right, Gina. We are so proud of you. And that doesn't mean we won't continue to worry. You know we are going to bug you with our calls and texts. But we have faith in you. Just continue to rely on God who will get you through this as he has thus far."

"I miss them. I miss them every day. I love Alex. But I miss them so much."

Maria cradled her daughter's head in her lap, stroked her hair and told her she always would. But that each day it would get a little easier.

Her Dad got up from the table, leaving his daughter and wife alone, and went upstairs where Christian was rocking Alex.

"Sal." Christian was shocked to see him there and immediately could tell he wanted to talk to him about something serious.

He came right out with it. "You care for my daughter, correct?"

All he could do was nod.

"I'm counting on you to take care of her. Don't let me down, son. And don't let that mother of yours hurt her. If you do you will have to answer to me."

"Yes, sir."

"And one more thing. The tension between you two is thick and I can tell you don't know how to act around her. Just be yourself. Things will go back to normal."

Christian just prayed he was right.

~

Two days later, Christian kept his promise to Gina's father. He pulled up to her house after work and knocked on the door. When she opened it and looked at him questioningly, he walked right in. He couldn't help but look around the room and notice the disarray.

"What are you doing here, Christian? Yes, I know it's a mess. It's been a rough couple of days. I realized how much my mother had been doing keeping this place clean while cooking and cleaning and helping with the baby."

"What can I do?"

She relaxed instantly. "Can you stay with Alex

while I go take a shower? I haven't been able to take one since they left.

"Is something wrong with him?"

"No, he has just been a little fussy and when he sleeps, I don't care about a shower anymore—all I want to do is sleep."

"Then that's what you should do. But you need to let us help when you need it. That's why I'm here. I got this. Go take a shower—a long one. And do whatever you need to do up there. Sleep, clean, read a book. I don't care. I'm here for the duration."

"Thank you."

"Have you eaten?"

"No, every time I go to heat something up Alex cries and then I never get back to it. But my Mom left a ton of stuff."

"I'll heat something up for us when you come back downstairs.

"Thank you, Chris."

"You're welcome."

~

About an hour later Gina walked downstairs to see Alex happily swaying in his baby swing while Christian finished picking up all the baby items that were strewn along the floor. He also cleaned up the kitchen and heated up some of the food her Mom had left. A few minutes later they were sitting down to a wonderful meal.

"Have you been anywhere since your parents left?"

"Nope."

"I'm taking you out tomorrow."

"What?"

"It could be to Target for all I care. For a coffee.

You name it. But you have to get out of this house. We can take Alex with us."

She didn't argue with him. She just knew it would be easier because he would be with her.

"I can get off at 4 tomorrow. I will be over then."

"Sounds good."

~

The next day the three of them were walking around Target, Alex in his baby carrier in the front of the cart, and Gina walking around adding mainly baby related items. Gina was smiling and did seem to be happy to be out of the house, until they rounded the corner and ran into his parents. Helena looked at Gina, then at Christian and was uncharacteristically at a loss for words so it was John who broke the silence by immediately honing in on the baby.

"Look how precious. Oh, Gina he is already getting so big. How are you doing, dear?"

"I'm good. My parents just left two days ago. They were a huge help but the two of us are adjusting nicely. Your son has been a big help. It was his idea to get us out of the house today."

"Shouldn't you still be at work, Christian?" said his mother.

"Easy, Mom, you know I have flexible hours."

"I just don't want you wasting your time and getting yourself into trouble."

"Mom, stop!" then Alex started fussing.

"I think that's our cue to go," said John. You two have a great rest of your day." Gina wasn't surprised how quick John was to sweep the awkwardness under the rug. But who was she to talk as she stood there in silence? They walked away and Gina opened her purse and grabbed her credit card.

"Chris, will you pay for these things for me? I'm going to take the baby to the car, and we will meet you there." Without waiting for him to answer she was gone.

Christian loaded her purchases in the trunk and got in. He didn't bother saying a word and wanted to see if Gina would say anything first but wasn't surprised when she didn't.

When she pulled in the house, he told her he would get the bags while she took the baby inside. Once all the packages were put away, and Alex was out of his car seat and lying on the floor happily looking at the objects around him, Alex started.

"Why didn't you say anything to her?"

Was he really blaming her for this?

"Excuse me?"

"You can't let everyone keep fighting your battles for you."

"Fighting my battles? I'm sorry what did you do today to stand up to your mother? What did your Dad do? Do you really want me to scream at her in Target? I won't give her the satisfaction."

"You can't let her treat you like that."

"Go."

"Gina."

"Get out right now."

"You don't have any problem standing up to me. Why can't you do the same to my mother?"

"You respect me, Christian. At least I thought you did. It's totally different. I'm not going to war with your mother. And I don't think Alex would want me to."

"What else would Alex want?" as he stepped closer.

"Not this," and she opened the door for him again and said good night.

She texted Elizabeth immediately. "Come over and bring wine."

"On my way."

"What's the emergency," she asked her best friend as she walked in with a bottle of Pinot Grigio.

"The Andros clan."

"Any one in particular?

"Well, I saw three of them today, except Anna. She may be the only sane one in the family.

"Okay I want to hear all about it but first I want to make sure you are good with the wine. I noticed you haven't had any since …"

The words hung in the air.

"I know. But I would like a glass now just to calm down. As you can see there is none in my house and I don't plan on buying any. If we don't finish this, I want you to take it back with you. Deal?"

"Deal. Now spill. Who did what this time?"

She recounted the story, and it was Elizabeth who reached for the bottle and poured herself another glass. Gina waved her hand away when Elizabeth gestured to Gina asking if she wanted more.

"Well, I'm glad you told me to bring wine because I needed it."

"Right?"

"So, tell me about your feelings for Christian."

Gina almost spit out the mouthful she had just swallowed.

"Really, that's what you ask me? What about my horrible ex mother-in-law?"

"Well, if you and Christian ever admit your feelings

for each other there will be nothing ex about it."

"Elizabeth!"

"Come on, Gina. How does he make you feel?"

"Safe. Happy. Exasperated!"

Elizabeth rolled her eyes.

"And I can't separate him from Alex. I really can't. I look at him and all I see is my dead husband and half the time it just makes me sad."

"I'm sorry, Gina. And I'm sorry I pushed."

"It's okay. And it would never work anyway--not when Helena hates me so much. I have to keep away from that woman. It's not healthy for me."

"What do you mean?"

"I mean I haven't had a drink in how long and today I see her and go for the wine?"

"You are right. When is your next grief meeting?"

"I am glad you asked. It's tomorrow night and it's the first time my parents aren't here to watch Alex. I really don't want to miss it. Can you watch him?"

"Of course. Let's make it a standard babysitting date."

~

Gina walked in the room, immediately spotted Grace and broke into a huge smile. She had missed her so much and already felt better just by seeing her. She walked over and took the seat Grace always saved for her.

When it was time for the sharing part of the night, Gina's hand shot up the fastest. Funny how things had changed.

She recounted the story from Target and what Christian said to her—that she needed to stand up to Helena.

"What do you think about that?" Dr. Roberts asked.

"I just don't understand what he wants me to do."

"Why do you think he gets so angry about it?"

She really tried to think hard on that but came up with nothing.

"Think, Gina. Why is he so angry with his mother about how she is treating you?"

"I don't know. Maybe because he thinks she has no reason to be mad at me about the accident?"

"Do you think Helena has a reason to be angry?"

For the first time she really seemed to consider that question and for once come up with the right answer.

"I don't."

"Why not?" She tried not to notice that every eye in the room was on her.

"Because I did nothing wrong."

"Hallelujah! Amen!" said Grace from the chair next to her and those in the room who knew her story cheered.

The truth seemed to finally dawn on her. "I did nothing wrong. She needs to stop blaming me for a horrible accident that wasn't my fault. I can't keep taking on that guilt. I need to let it go."

Grace squeezed her hand and Gina wondered why it took her nearly a year to come to that realization.

~

After Elizabeth left the house Gina texted Christian and apologized for it being so late but asked if he could come over.

"On my way."

When she opened the door, she took his hand and pulled him inside then let it go. "I'm so sorry, Christian."

"There's nothing …"

"Stop. I need to say this. I had a breakthrough tonight at grief group. I know now that the accident wasn't my fault."

He took her hand back and let her continue.

"I know that now. And you know what? Now I'm mad."

He looked at her quizzically.

"I'm mad that I have let your mother treat me this way. I am mad that I took on the guilt she gave me and carried it with me. I know now that it's not my fault and I am ready to let it go."

"So what are you going to do?"

She knew what he was alluding to.

"Nothing. But if I see her again, and she treats me as she has in the past, I am letting her know this is not my guilt to carry. If she wants to blame me that is her choice but I'm not accepting it anymore. I want to live my life and enjoy the blessing that God has given me in my beautiful baby boy."

All he could do was pull her in for a hug and tell her how proud he was of her.

~

Grace and Elizabeth had been texting each other back and forth in dreaded anticipation of the day coming up in one week—the day of the accident. No one was mentioning it but the two women conversed about how they all must be thinking about it. They didn't want to bring it up to Christian and Anna as it would be a tough day for them. And they certainly weren't going to broach it with Gina—though they decided she must be thinking about it.

"I think we should tell her we are coming over for a

girl's night on that day," Elizabeth texted Grace.

"Sounds like a plan."

Elizabeth sent it off in a group text among the three of them and waited for a reply.

"I want to be alone that day," Gina said. "But I love you both for thinking of me."

"We can't let you, Gina. Sorry but we will be there with comfort food galore. Prayers. Listening. Whatever you need from us we will give you but we are sorry we just can't leave you alone," said Elizabeth.

"Agree," texted Grace. In fact, I'm coming over early. I can watch Alex all day. You can sleep through it for all I care. But I'm coming. And if you don't answer, be prepared that I will let myself in."

Gina didn't send a response. She knew it was impossible to argue with Grace.

~

Three days before the dreaded date the tension in the Andros house was high as they all knew it was coming but no one wanted to talk about it. Helena was the one to bring it up at Sunday dinner.

"We need to talk about the plans for Wednesday."

Nobody moved.

"I have arranged for us to go to church at seven before everyone goes to work—though I don't know how any of you would be able to concentrate that day. Father Andino is going to hold a special mass and remember Alex and Teresa."

"That sounds very nice, Mom," said Christian. "Thank you for planning it."

"You're welcome. But, Christian, please don't ruin this by inviting Gina."

~

"Christian, what are you going to do?" asked Anna when they had left.

"About what?"

"Seriously? Are you going to invite Gina to mass?"

"I'm not. Now is not the time to add fuel to Mom's fire. I know she is being awful to her but I think on Wednesday we just need to let her grieve and be there for her at mass. We can go see Gina later."

"That's why you are the favorite you know." Anna said.

He swatted her and smiled, something he didn't expect anyone to do in a few days.

~

Grace knocked on Gina's door at seven Wednesday morning. She knew Alex was an early riser then went down for a nap around 8 so she didn't feel the least bit bad. When she didn't answer she started pounding until Gina finally let her in.

"You're annoying, you know that right?"

Grace could tell Gina had already been crying and she simply took her in her arms until Gina finally let go when Alex started to whimper.

"So, where's the junk food?"

Grace smiled. "Well for breakfast I have croissants with raspberry jam and some donut holes."

"That will do for now," Gina said.

Grace started unpacking the items and asked if she could pray before they ate, and Gina nodded.

"Dear, Lord, thank you for bringing Gina this far and holding her in the palm of your hand. But you know how hard this day will be and we need you Lord. Look over Gina, and all of the Andros family, as they grieve their losses today. You are the only one who can get them through this. We ask this all in your precious name Amen."

"Amen," Gina said, then squeezed Grace's hand and ran to the bathroom to dry all her tears.

Alex started to fuss right after Gina finished her croissant and a few donuts.

"You know how you said you would watch Alex today?"

"Yes, answered Grace."

"Well, can you take him while I go hide under my pillow and wallow?"

"Of course, as long as you come out for the comfort food lunch I am preparing."

"You got it."

"And I will be checking on you."

"I don't doubt it."

~

The mass was beautiful but Christian didn't think it really did anything to numb his pain. He and Anna had decided to go to work today only because they hoped keeping busy would help them get through this horrible date on the calendar. Christian felt like Gina was on his mind every second. He didn't want to bug her as he knew Grace was there but he would check on her later.

~

Grace opened the door to Gina's room and saw her lying in the fetal position fully covered, minus a few black patches of hair sticking out of her white down comforter. She walked over and sat down, pulled down the cover slightly and stroked her hair.

"Are you ready for some lunch?"

"Not really. How's Alex?"

"He's doing great," said Grace, secretly pleased

Gina asked about him. "Why don't you come down and spend a little time with him. I am sure he will make you smile—and I can make you my famous grilled-cheese sandwich."

"I'll try in a little bit."

"Okay but know that if I don't see you soon, I'm coming back up here."

Gina sat up suddenly in bed, surprising Grace.

"Are Elizabeth and Anna still coming over later?"

"They are."

"Can't you just tell them I'm okay?"

"Are you?"

"I'm not, but I don't want to have to talk to anyone today. Please Grace. I love them but please can you tell them to stay away."

"Gina, you have been doing so great we can't let you slide down into this grief pit again."

"I won't."

"How do you know? If you stay there today, how are you going to just flip the switch and be different tomorrow? You won't. We won't let that happen to you Gina. Someone needs to be with you, and I have to leave later tonight."

"Fine, but I'm staying here in bed. Give Alex a kiss for me." Then she pulled the covers back up over her head, resuming her initial position.

~

Elizabeth pulled up in Anna's driveway as they had planned to drive to Gina's together. Anna's grief was evident from the minute she opened the car door. Elizabeth leaned over and gave her a hug and the tears she kept at bay all day finally started to flow.

"I can't do it."

"What?"

"I can't go over there and comfort Gina. I just can't. I'm too much of a mess today."

Elizabeth leaned over again and hugged her friend. "Then you won't. You have to heal also, Anna. Why don't I drop you at Christian's? Or at your Mom and Dad's? I will go check on Gina tonight."

"Are you sure?"

"Absolutely. And I will call or text you later to check in on you too."

~

Elizabeth finally showed up at Gina's right before Grace had to leave and the older woman delivered a quick rundown and reported that Gina was still in bed where she had been all day.

"Thanks, Grace. I owe you."

"No problem at all. It's a rough day but our girl will be okay," and then she left looking older than she had when Elizabeth saw her last week.

Elizabeth walked upstairs to Gina's room with Alex in her arms thinking maybe that would bring her back to the land of the living. Gina turned in the bed when she heard Alex cry.

"You don't have to be here," said Gina.

"Actually, from the look of things I really think I do."

"Where's Anna?"

"I dropped her with her family. She was a mess."

Gina was silent and Elizabeth wondered if Gina was realizing others were in pain as well including two of her best friends who just happened to be her sister and brother-in-law.

"Go away."

"I won't. Alex needs his Mom," then she lay him on the bed next to Gina and went downstairs announcing dinner would be ready in 30 minutes.

Gina and Alex came downstairs exactly 30 minutes later to a home-cooked dinner that Elizabeth had brought and must have heated up at Gina's. Garlic bread, chicken parmesan and salad—all of Gina's favorites. They ate in relative silence but that was fine with Elizabeth, she was just glad her friend came out of her room.

"Have you talked to either of them today," Elizabeth asked.

"What do you think?"

"I think you haven't, but that surprises me given the fact that they have been here for you over the past few months. Maybe today you show up for them."

Gina picked up Alex and walked upstairs wishing Elizabeth wasn't right but knowing she was.

She texted them both. "I just wanted to let you know I am thinking of you on this awful day. Love you and hope you are okay."

They both texted back saying they were at Christian's and that she should come over. No part of her wanted to but she knew she should, so she walked downstairs, gave Elizabeth a huge hug and told her she was right and that she was off the hook.

Gina knocked on Christian's door with baby in tow and a bag of junk food Grace had left for her. They both came to answer it, face wet with tears.

"I brought reinforcements. The baby who will make you smile, and junk food that will bring you limited instant gratification. And me to give you hugs and thank you for being the best friends ever and letting me be here with you on this difficult day."

That's all it took for Anna to break down. "I miss him so much. Every scene from our childhood keeps running through my head. Your wedding. The day Teresa was born. I don't know how you are surviving this Gina because I don't know that I can."

Christian and Gina took her in their arms and let her cry and then Chris started right along with his sister.

"You can, Anna. You have been and you will. You have been telling me how strong I am, and you are just as strong--way more than me. You will get through this. We all will."

Anna looked up at both of them. "You know what might help?"

"What?"

"Those chips you brought in." Gina laughed and went to open the bag and brought it over to the couch.

"So, did you two work today?"

"We did," said Christian. "But Mom had a mass for Alex and Teresa this morning, so we went there first."

"How was it?"

"It was nice," said Anna. "It didn't really make us feel any better but it was important to Mom."

"I'm sorry, Gina we don't have to talk about this."

"No way are you guys going to not talk about your mother in front of me. We may not be on speaking terms right now but she's your mother and I don't want you acting differently around me because of it."

"Right now?" said Anna. "So you really still think there is hope?"

"Where God is there is always hope."

Chapter 18

Two weeks after the dreaded anniversary date, Christian texted Gina. "Dinner out tonight? Anna is dying to watch Alex and it will give you a break. I won't let you say no."

"What time?" she texted back though still terrified as she still hadn't had many trips out of the house since that awful doctor visit.

"I'll be there at seven."

"Where are we going?"

"It's a surprise. Dress nice."

Two hours later she decided it has been almost a year since she had dressed nice. And the last time she did Alex was still alive. In fact, she had probably done it for him. What was she doing? She knew Christian and she were just going out as friends but still … it felt different. The doorbell rang and Gina ran to the door still dressed in her sweats and baggy t-shirt.

"Gina! Isn't my brother picking you up in like 20 minutes?"

"I have nothing to wear. I can't do it."

She looked over at Alex where he was sleeping soundly in his playpen then took Gina by the arm and led her upstairs. By the time Anna was done Gina was wearing one of her favorite red dresses, black heels and her hair piled up on a bun with simple gold hoop earrings. Anna had also done her makeup and she looked beautiful.

"Anna, it's too much."

"It's not! When is the last time you have dressed up? Before you had Alex? Wouldn't you say it's about time?"

Before she could answer the doorbell rang.

"It's too late to back out now, Gina. Go get it. I'll take care of Alex. You have a great time and don't rush back to us."

Gina opened the door and stared. Christian was wearing black slacks and a fitted gray shirt and a red tie which matched her dress.

"Well, look at us with our matching red," was all he said while he couldn't stop thinking about how beautiful she looked.

She smiled. "You better be taking me someplace good that makes it worth all the primping your sister put me through."

"Oh, it will be worth it," he said while walking past her to get a glimpse of Alex before they left.

"Have fun, sis."

"You know I will. I can't wait to snuggle with this guy. You kids have fun."

They pulled up to Antonio's—her favorite Italian place and broke into a huge grin. "Okay, it was worth it."

"That's it? Wow, you make it easy for a guy."

She looked at him quizzically but ignored that comment, while he came over to the driver's side to open her door. As they walked toward the restaurant, she prayed they wouldn't run into anyone they knew— and then she spied Helena and John through the window. She quickly grabbed Christian's arm and dragged him down the street, away from the restaurant.

"Gina, what's wrong?"

"Your mother and father are in there. Let's just go home."

He cursed silently. "Gina. I promised you a night out, which you so deserve and I'm giving it to you."

"Vinny's," they both said in unison, and walked back to the car.

"I'm really sorry, Gina. I will take you to Antonio's another day."

"You better. But you know we are way too dressed up for Vinny's. But guess what? I don't care." Inwardly she was relieved as the idea of going to the fancy restaurant with Chris had her a little on edge.

"We can class up the joint. And Vinny will be so excited, as he is always asking about you." Immediately he saw her stiffen.

"Gina, it's okay. You have to start going out and seeing people you haven't seen since Alex has been gone. It will get easier each time. That is one of the reasons I wanted to bring you out tonight."

"Doesn't it bother you, Christian?"

"Not anymore. I am past all that awkwardness now. But yes it will be hard for you because you have been shutting yourself off. But I will be here to help you." And he took her hand and led her inside.

Vinny tried to hide his shock when he saw Gina and Christian walk in together. They almost looked like Gina and Alex, especially with Christian holding her hand. As soon as Gina saw Vinny look at the two of them, she dropped his hand. To break the awkwardness, she walked up to the restaurant owner and drew him in a huge hug. "Long time no see."

"I've missed you so much, Gina. But it's made me feel better to know you are still eating my food when Christian and his sister come pick it up for you."

She smiled. "There is no way I could have gone that long without your lasagna or your eggplant!"

"Why are you kids all dolled up tonight just to come to my humble establishment?"

"Gina needed a night out so I told her to dress up."

"Well, you look beautiful. Can you do me a favor?"

"Anything."

"Next time you come in can you bring Alex Jr. with you? I hear he's a looker."

She looked at Christian who grinned sheepishly. "Of course."

"Great, I am sure you all are starving. Let me take you to your table."

Gina was already relaxed when not a few minutes earlier she wanted to bolt back to the comfort of her home where she didn't have to worry about sympathetic looks and curious stares. But Christian was right--she had to get out sometimes. She was just glad he was here to help her do it.

"You look happy."

"I am. Thanks, Chris for getting me out tonight. Once again you were right."

"I'm sorry, what was that?"

She reached across the table and swatted him playfully.

"Be sure to remember that next time. Because I am definitely taking you out again."

"Okay, but we are going to Antonio's. And you are finding out your parents schedule to be sure they won't be there."

He just nodded his head, and she regretted her words.

"I'm sorry, Christian. They are your parents. I shouldn't have said that. I don't want to put you in a weird position."

"Stop. It's not you—you know that. Don't you think I feel awful to see what my mother is doing to you? And my Dad—I mean he doesn't agree with it and yes they fight about it, but does he really do anything to stop it?"

"Come on. You know as well as I do there is nothing John can do. I'm sorry I upset you. Can we just enjoy our night?"

He silently cursed his mother. He tried to tell himself she was grieving too but she had never acted like this with anyone before—he never thought it would happen with Gina of all people. He so wished they could still all get together for their Sunday dinner, doting over Alex Jr., Gina helping his Mom in the kitchen.

"Christian."

"Sorry. Yes, let's talk about something else. Next week I am going to Vegas for work did I tell you that?"

She didn't remember. "When do you leave?"

"Sunday. Gina, what is it?"

"Nothing. I will just miss you. And that scares me. I

can't depend on you like that, Chris. Or anyone."

He could sense her getting agitated and he just wanted to take her hand and tell her he would always be there for her. But she wasn't ready for that--brother-in-law or not. She was feeling like she could only depend on herself. It's the walls she put up after Alex's death and he couldn't blame her for it. He let out a sigh of relief when he saw the waiter coming over with their food to break the awkwardness in the air.

After their meal, they discussed safe subjects, the latest milestones for Alex Jr., Anna and Elizabeth. Gina told him her parents were due for a visit in a few weeks. Then the conversation died down and he knew it was time to take her home.

~

A few days later Gina was back in her sweats and getting more stressed by the minute. Alex had been so fussy since the day before and it seemed there was nothing she could do to calm him down. All his crying made her realize he was a pretty easy baby—nothing like Teresa was. She had colic and Alex and Gina always had to take turns consoling her each night as that was the time it was always at its worst. When she looked back at it now, when she thought she was so stressed, she would go back to that time in a second. When Alex would come over and take Teresa from her and tell her to go take a bath, to relax, that he would take care of their little Angel. It seemed like such a hard time but if she only knew what was to come.

She took Alex upstairs to the rocker and tried to soothe him but nothing seemed to work. If he didn't feel better, she would have to call the doctor in the morning. She had a feeling it was going to be a long night. She just wished her husband were here to help her through it.

Gina woke the next morning trying to figure out how much sleep they both got—maybe two hours, if that. She felt his forehead—no fever and she didn't know why he was so inconsolable, so she called the doctor and made an appointment for a few hours later.

The doctor took one look at Gina and was concerned. "Gina, are you taking care of yourself?"

"I am. I swear. I know I look awful now but really, I have been good. But he has cried for the past day, maybe we got two hours of sleep last night. I don't know what's wrong with him. I can't lose him," and she immediately started crying, the stress of the last 24 hours catching up with her.

"Gina, you aren't going to lose him," and immediately became concerned. "Have you asked your friends for help? This is the time you need to lean on then. The baby can feel your stress. Call a friend to come take him for a little bit while you go take a nap. You aren't doing either of you any good this way."

"What's wrong with him?"

"Let's take a look."

He cried a lot while the doctor examined him which actually made Gina feel a little better. At least it wasn't her.

"His ears are pretty inflamed indicating an ear infection and that would explain all the screaming. I will give him an antibiotic and you should start to see some results."

"Thank you."

"You're welcome. And Gina--he will still be cranky for a day or two. Call your friends. It's okay to ask for help you know."

She nodded and walked as fast as she could out of the office.

Thank goodness Alex fell asleep on the way home. She carried the car seat into the house praying he would stay that way. She would be happy with a twenty-minute nap. He seemed to listen, so she placed the car seat next to the couch and lie down until his cries woke her about an hour later. He seemed to calm down after his bottle, so when he swayed happily in his swing she texted Christian. "Want to come over tonight?"

"Just landed in Vegas."

"Shoot, I forgot. Have fun."

She didn't feel like asking anyone else to help her and tried not to dissect that decision. She looked over at Alex nodding off again and she stretched out and fell asleep along with him.

~

Two days later she woke up to Alex wailing, and immediately could tell he had a fever when she touched him to pick him up. When she took his temperature, it was 102. It was late Sunday night so she couldn't call the doctor. Should she go to the emergency room? That seemed silly as the doctor said it was an ear infection, but he just wouldn't stop crying and now the fever. It seemed the whole world was busy. She called her Mom, Elizabeth, Anna, Grace, no one was answering. What were they all doing on a Sunday night? She knew she had to get him to the hospital so she packed him up in his car seat and went to the car but it wouldn't start and she started sobbing uncontrollably.

She took Alex back in the house and there was literally no one else to call so she called John's cell but there was no answer. She dialed the house praying with all her might that Helena wouldn't pick up.

"Hello?"

"Helena, is John home?"

"He isn't. He is working the night shift tonight. What's wrong? Why is Alex crying so bad?"

"I don't know but he has a fever and I need to take him to the hospital and my car won't start and no one is home," she said fighting back the tears with everything she had.

"I will be right there," and she hung up.

When Helena knocked on the door, Gina let her in then strapped Alex into his car seat. "Thank you for coming. When did you learn to drive?"

"I can drive I just choose not to. Are you okay to drive my car to the hospital?"

"Of course."

After Gina got the car seat installed, they drove in mostly silence. Helena asked a few questions about Alex and Gina filled her in on what the doctor had said. Gina parked, got checked in then unbuckled Alex from his car seat and tried to console him but nothing helped. The others in the emergency room waiting area sent her looks of sympathy. She looked at Helena who seemed to sense her question.

"Let me try. I know you are stressed and probably have had no sleep over the past few days."

"Thank you."

Alex really wouldn't calm down for Helena either, but she wasn't as stressed out as Gina, so it helped a little. They were finally called back to a waiting area and Alex's cries seemed to get worse and when Helena got close to Gina Alex seemed to reach out to her, so she took him in her arms. Helena watched as Gina walked around the small room with him, whispered in his ear, sang him songs and was able to soothe him for small periods of time, all while looking absolutely exhausted.

The doctor finally came back and examined him and said it was a good thing Gina brought him in. The ear infections had gotten worse, so the doctor inferred this particular medication wasn't working. She wanted to give him a dose of another antibiotic here at the hospital and keep them here for a few hours to see if he calmed down.

"I'll be back in a few hours. I'm sorry to keep you here but I really would like to check him out again before I discharge you."

"I appreciate it, doctor. You may just want to warn the other patients about the wailing."

She laughed. "I think they will survive." She started to walk away, then said, "I can tell you are a really good mom. I know this is frustrating but you are doing a great job and I just thought you needed to hear that right now."

"I did," and again she held back the tears. She refused to cry in front of Helena.

"Would you like me to take him?" Helena asked.

"Thank you," and she passed him over.

"Why don't you lie down, gesturing to the bed, "and try to rest."

~

John came home in his police car and noticed the car was gone and immediately got worried. He went in the house and couldn't find Helena anywhere. He texted Christian and Anna and no one knew where she was and his wife wasn't answering her cell. Where could she be?

~

Gina pulled in her driveway with Alex and Helena around midnight. The doctor told her it seemed the new antibiotic was working, and Alex should be less fussy in a few days. Gina knew she should be happy, but immediately wondered how she was going to get through two more days of this. Again, she ached for her husband.

"I'm going to stay here tonight," Helena said as she followed Gina in the house. "Is that okay? I want you to be able to get some rest so I can help with the baby."

Gina nodded and walked over to the couch and pulled the blanket tight.

"Don't you want to go upstairs?"

"Too tired. Helena?"

"Yes?"

"Are you going to take him away from me?"

Helena couldn't speak for a minute, unable to comprehend what Gina just asked.

"Why would you ask that?"

"You tried to get custody. Why wouldn't you just take him back to your house if you still think I'm not a fit mother?"

Helena walked up to Gina, knelt next to her on the couch so their faces were inches apart. Before she said anything, the tears were already forming in her eyes.

"Gina, I am so sorry for everything I have done to you. You are a wonderful mother. You always have been. I am so sorry," she said, while sobbing fully now. "I don't know if what I did was forgivable but do you think one day you could forgive me for everything I have done to you?"

"I already have."

Helena kissed her on the cheek, and she fell asleep.

~

John was full on frantic now and he had his two children in a panic right along with him. Then he heard his phone ring and saw his wife's name come up on the screen.

"Helena, where have you been? We are all worried sick."

"It's a long story, John but I'm okay and I won't be home until sometime tomorrow. Are you sitting down?"

"I am now."

"I'm at Gina's."

~

John couldn't believe it, and neither could Christian when he relayed the story to him after hanging up with Helena.

"I don't even know what to say," said Christian. "All I can say is that Gina has been right all along."

"What do you mean?"

"God does answer prayer."

Christian reasoned there was no other explanation for what had just happened. He couldn't believe he had three more days in Vegas until he could get home and see this reconciliation in person. Maybe then he would really believe it.

~

When Christian finally got back, he texted Gina and found out her parents were visiting, and she asked if he could wait a few days before coming over. Was she kidding? Didn't she know how much this was killing him and he had to hear all about what had transpired while he was away?

"Sure," was all he could say in response. "Text me when they are gone."

He was actually relieved tomorrow was Sunday so he could get the full story from his mother during Sunday dinner. It couldn't get here fast enough.

~

Gina had told her parents what happened with Helena when they arrived two days ago. Sal told Maria she should be thrilled but Maria was skeptical and worried about her daughter. She just didn't want to see her get hurt again. Sal had the same worries but told his wife they had to trust that God's hand was in all of this.

~

They sat at the kitchen table drinking coffee Sunday morning when the phone rang. Maria didn't want Gina and Alex to wake up, so she grabbed the phone on the second ring.

"Hello."

"Maria?"

"Yes."

"It's Helena."

Maria didn't respond but was looking at her husband with pure shock on her face.

"First, let me apologize for the way I have treated your daughter. I am deeply sorry and only hope that one day your family can forgive me. I have asked God for forgiveness as well."

"I appreciate that, Helena," was all she could muster, while Sal registered surprise when he heard who it was on the other end of the phone.

"I wanted to know if all of you wanted to come over today for dinner."

"Sure, that would be nice," she said not knowing what else to say.

"Great, see you at four?"

"Sure, thank you."

"I look forward to seeing all of you."

"Well, Sal. I guess we are going to Sunday dinner at the Andros' tonight."

~

Maria was holding baby Alex in Gina's room while her daughter was getting ready. She knew Gina all too well and could tell she was anxious.

"How do I look?"

"You look great, Gina," Maria said, looking at her in her black knit shirt and dark denim jeans. "How do you feel about this?"

"I'm nervous. I haven't really talked to her since Alex was sick. I haven't seen Christian or Anna. I just don't know how this is going to go but I have to leave it in God's hands," she said matter-of-factly while placing some simple gold hoops in her ears.

"I'm so glad she apologized but you have to tread carefully."

"I know, Mom. I love you. Thanks for taking care of me."

"Always."

~

Christian and Anna got to their parent's house at their normal time of three and after greeting their Dad headed to say hello to their Mom who they knew would be prepping in the kitchen. Their normally perfectly mother seemed to be a little frazzled.

"Hey, Mom," they both said in unison.

Before she could answer Christian noticed she was

prepping way more food than usual.

"Are you expecting more than just us?" asked Christian.

"That's a ton of food there," added Anna, looking at the large pan of eggplant parmesan in the baking pan.

"I am. Gina, the baby and her parents will be here at four."

The siblings just looked at each other.

"Listen. I know your father gave you the quick rundown on what happened. There are a lot of people that have to forgive me for what I have done and that will take time. And that includes you two. I am so sorry I made you turn away from her. I'm just sorry for everything and I hope one day you can forgive me."

They both took their mother in their arms.

"Of course, Mom," said Anna.

"Now listen I have a lot of food to prep. I am sure today will have its awkward moments but I'm trying. This is my olive branch and I just hope that in time everyone can reach out and take it."

~

An hour later the doorbell rang, and Helena yelled that she would answer the door so the rest of the family stayed in the family room, not knowing what else to do and figuring they would just take their cues from her.

"Hello, Gina," she said, greeting her with a kiss on the cheek.

"Sal. Maria. Thank you so much for coming."

"Thank you for having us," said Sal while moving into the house to greet the rest of the family.

Once everyone had said hello Maria couldn't help but notice that the photos of Gina and Alex on their wedding day were back up on the wall. All the ones with her daughter in it that were gone several months ago were again in their proper place. Maria just hoped it was for good but was skeptical. She had to watch out for Gina who just couldn't take any more hurt and betrayal. But she was proud of her. Maria knew a huge weight had been lifted off of her when Helena asked for forgiveness, but watching her now talking to Helena, she knew she was being careful and that made her proud. Gina seemed to be getting stronger every day.

Sal was taking in the room as well. And the big thing he noticed was that Christian couldn't take his eyes off his daughter.

~

"Before we head into dinner, I just want to thank you all for coming," said Helena, way less confident than she usually appeared. "And I want to thank you all for meeting me halfway. Sal, Maria. I feel awful for how I treated Gina and hope one day you can forgive me."

"Thank you, Helena," said Maria.

"We appreciate your efforts," said Sal. "And we do forgive you."

And with that everyone headed to the table with Christian eyeing the spot next to Gina and praying no one else would claim it. When no one did, and Gina wasn't yet seated, he pulled out the chair for her.

"Helena?"

"Yes, Gina?"

"Would you mind if I prayed?"

"I would love it."

They all bowed their heads.

"Dear, Lord, thank you for bringing all of us together today and for allowing us to share in this beautiful meal Helena has so kindly prepared. Please bless this food we are about to eat. And thank you for having your hand in all of our lives and helping us all to heal. And please bless those not here with us today but up in heaven. In your name we pray, Amen."

"Amen," said everyone around the table in unison, all of them fighting back tears.

Everyone was perfectly polite at dinner, but after when they started cleaning up and then gathered in the living room, they were more relaxed and at ease. Alex had been passed from arm to arm and was back to his sweet self, only crying when he had to be changed, fed or was really tired. Now was one of those times as he was off his schedule today due to not getting the long nap, he usually took each afternoon.

"Well, that's my cue," Gina said. "I think this little guy needs to get home and get ready for bed. Helena, thank you so much for a lovely day."

"You are very welcome. I loved having all of you here."

"Yes, thank you, Helena," said Maria. "I'm not sure when we will see you again as we are headed back home on Tuesday."

"Well, I look forward to seeing you on your next visit, whenever that may be."

"Actually, I wanted to tell everyone something," said Gina. "I've been starting to think about getting Alex baptized soon. "I'm talking to my pastor about setting a date."

"Oh, Gina that is wonderful," said her mother.

"We will definitely be back for that," said Sal.

Gina hugged everyone else goodbye and when she got to Christian, he whispered in her ear. "Antonio's this week. Not taking no for an answer. Dress nice."

She looked at him and smiled and the whole room noticed, they all just wondered when Gina was going to figure out what the rest of them already knew.

Chapter 19

Two days later, her parents were gone, and Elizabeth was over for a girl's night. Gina had finally caught her up on the events from the past two weeks.

"I can't even believe all of this has happened."

"I know," said Gina smiling and Elizabeth noticed her friend was almost back to her old self again. She would always be different in light of everything that happened but she was starting to enjoy life again.

"Elizabeth, I want to ask you something. I have set a date for Alex's baptism and I really want you to be the Godmother.

"I can't."

Gina nearly spit out her drink.

"What do you mean?"

"I'm assuming you are asking Christian to be the Godfather?"

"I am."

"Then you have to ask Anna. Gina, I love you. But this is Alex's baby and it just makes sense that his siblings, who happen to be the Aunt and Uncle, both be the Godparents. You know that too."

"But you are my best friend."

"And I know you don't want to hear this now. Maybe it's two years or five years, maybe less than that, I don't know. But one day you are going to find someone, and you will be a mother yet again and I call dibs. I am definitely the Godmother of that child."

"Are you sure?" Gina didn't know what else to say.

"Absolutely, and you know I'm right."

She did and silently thanked the Lord for giving her such an amazing best friend. As for that soon to be named father of her next baby, Gina could only imagine one person who interested her even though she knew it was wrong.

"So, when Anna gets here later are you going to ask her?"

"If you don't mind."

"Not at all. I can't wait to see how happy she is."

An hour later they were all catching up with Anna, again marveling at the events of the past few weeks. Even Anna was shocked at the change of heart her mother had made.

"Anna, did you know Gina set a date to baptize Alex?"

"Oh my gosh, Gina that's awesome. Let me know what you need me to do to help."

"I will take you up on that but I also want to ask you something. Will you be Alex's Godmother?"

Her eyes filled up with tears and she looked from Elizabeth to Gina. "But ..."

"I would like you and Christian to be the Godparents to your nephew. Elizabeth says she understands."

"Are you sure?" said Anna.

"I am."

"And so am I," said Elizabeth. But I already called dibs on Gina's next baby," and they all laughed.

"Then I would be honored."

"Don't say anything to Christian yet. I am seeing him tomorrow and will ask him then."

"What are you guys doing?" asked Anna, even though she already knew Christian was taking her to Antonio's. She hoped Christian would be the person Gina would eventually end up with but she knew Gina wasn't ready to admit that yet.

"We are going to dinner."

"So what are you going to wear?"

"I'm actually glad you asked. I have to dress up and again I am at a total loss."

"Then let's go raid your closet." And the three of them headed upstairs.

~

Grace rang the doorbell the next day as she was watching Alex so Gina could go out with Christian. But she was coming over a little early to get the scoop on all the recent events. Grace had stayed away to let Gina spend time with her parents while they were visiting though they continued to see each other each week at grief group.

"Gina, you look amazing." She was wearing a lovely hunter green dress that suited her coloring perfectly. This time she wore her hair down in loose curls draping her shoulders.

"So, what time will Christian be here?"

"He just texted that he is running a little late so

about 30 minutes."

"Perfect. Come sit and give me the scoop."

Gina filled Grace in on a few of the details she had missed. She knew Grace now talked with Elizabeth and Anna somewhat regularly, even if it was via text, so Gina knew they already gave her all the gossip.

"Actually, I have something for you, Grace." She walked over to the kitchen table and picked up an envelope. "It's from Helena. And I'll be honest. I'm dying to know what it says."

"Then let's find out," as she opened it and started reading.

"Dear, Grace. No one has ever talked to me the way you did at the hospital that day. Although I was furious at the time, I want to thank you and apologize for the way I have treated Gina. You were right, though it took me awhile to realize it. I will never forgive myself for not being there for her, but I thank God for all the people in her life who were—including you. I don't know much about your story but I know you have suffered deep loss of your own and have helped Gina immensely through her grief. I hope you can forgive me and that our paths will cross again soon so I can apologize in person. Helena Andros."

"Wow," was all Grace said at first. "God really does work in mysterious ways doesn't he?"

"Yes, he does," then the doorbell rang and Gina walked to the door with anticipation for the night that was to come.

~

Christian looked at Gina across the table and she looked even more beautiful than the first night they tried to come here. But then again Gina always looked radiant even in her sweats and baggy shirts. Nothing could ruin this night. So many great things have happened since then. The waiter came over to clear their plates and Gina knew it was the right time.

"Chris, I need to ask you something." He smiled every time she called him Chris.

"I finally set a date to baptize Alex. I know he is six months old already but everything is falling into place and this will be such a great event for the whole family to celebrate."

"That's so awesome, Gina."

"There's more. I have asked Anna to be the Godmother and I would like you to be the Godfather."

"Of course," he said fighting back tears. "I would be honored."

~

They left the restaurant and Christian asked Gina if she wanted to take a walk. He was finally ready to talk to her about his feelings though he was a nervous wreck. He took her hand and led her out of the restaurant down the path that led to the water where they could sit on the benches that lined the path. Gina was nervous now too but couldn't pinpoint why.

He still hadn't let go of her hand. "I would like to do this more with you, Gina."

She looked at him, not sure what he meant. "I want to take you out on a date—lots of dates. I want to pamper you as you deserve. I want to see you smile more. I want to hold your hand, talk to you at the end of every day."

He could feel the sweat coming harder now as she continued to stare at him without saying a word, so he kept going.

"You are my best friend, Gina. Do you think one day we could be something more? All I need to know right now if there is even a chance of us sometime in the future."

All she saw was Alex. Christian didn't even exist. She pictured them on their first date, then their second and third. All of her time with Alex ran through her mind and she had no idea how to respond.

"Are you surprised?"

"Not entirely."

"Do you feel anything for me besides friendship?"

She knew she did. The butterflies than ran through her when she saw one of his texts, or when he looked at her in that special way. But all she could see in front of her was Alex.

"I see a potential for more, yes."

He reached for her hand again but she pulled away.

"But right now, when I look at you all I see is Alex. I'm so sorry. I want to see you and only you. I'm just not there yet."

It's not what he wanted to hear but still it gave him hope.

He reached over and stroked her cheek, "I will be here whenever you are ready to see me in that new light. I want to show you how I feel about you. I want to help both of us heal together."

"What would your brother think?"

"I think he would be happy."

"I don't know how you could know that. And are you sure you don't have these feelings for me due to some unresolved devotion to your brother. Because I don't want your pity, Christian."

Now it was he who pulled away shifting away from

her on the bench.

"You really think that?"

"Maybe."

"So Alex is somehow making me light up every time I see you. Making me think of you more than I have ever thought of any girl I have ever dated?"

"Stop. Please. It's too much. Please take me home."

~

Christian pulled up in front of her house. Her plan was to get out of the car without saying goodbye, but it was Christian. She couldn't do that, so she turned toward him, and kissed him lightly on the cheek.

"I'm so sorry, Christian. I don't want to hurt you. You deserve so much better than me—more than your brother's damaged widow."

"Don't you think I should be able to decide what I deserve—who I want?"

"You are young, Christian. Go out and find someone to love—to have those first dates, to have a wedding, a child together, you don't want to be tied down by me and all this history and baggage."

"I want to have all of that with you. But I need you to know you are worthy of all that."

She closed the door and he drove away, and she felt the emptiness immediately.

The next few weeks went by in a blur. She missed him so much. Yes, there was all the drama after Alex died but when they reconnected it was so much stronger than before. She missed him every day, but didn't want to be the one to reach out—didn't want to lead him on though she wanted to see him so badly. She wondered if he thought of her as well.

~

"Christian, come on. Tell me what happened with Gina when you guys went out that night. Every time I have seen her since then she looks miserable and you look even worse. What happened?"

They were sitting on the couch in his apartment. He had been avoiding Anna for more than a week, so she finally stopped by unannounced.

"She looks miserable?"

"Yes! And I'm worried about her. I don't want her plunging into that bad place again. But she won't tell me anything either and I know it has something to do with the two of you."

"I told her I wanted to be more than friends."

Her heart immediately broke for him, as she could only imagine by the way he was acting that it didn't turn out as he had hoped.

"What did she say?"

"That maybe it could happen one day. But it won't. Because then she went on about how I just pity her as some debt she thinks I owe Alex."

She interrupted him. "Well did you tell her that wasn't true?"

He was silent.

"Christian! What did you tell her?"

"I don't know. She went on about how I should go out and find some nice girl with no baggage that I can go have kids with."

"Did you tell her you didn't want that?"

"I did. But then I told her she had to figure out she was worthy of all this and that when she was ready, I would be here."

"You didn't fight for her?"

He put his head in his hands suddenly knowing he

screwed up.

"Girls want reassurance. She wanted to hear that you wanted to be with her and only her. You gave up too easily. But I know why you did it."

"I didn't want to scare her!"

"I know," and she pulled him close.

"I didn't tell you the worst part. She told me she looks at me and all she sees is Alex."

"Ouch."

"Yeah. And then I guess after that I didn't feel like humiliating myself further. Now I can see that was wrong."

"You need to talk to her."

~

Anna left his house and although he knew he shouldn't do this by text he had to start somewhere.

"I'm sorry. What can I do to fix this? I miss you and don't want to lose you."

"I miss you too. Come over?"

"On my way."

~

She opened the door for him and immediately pulled him in for a long embrace. He inhaled the scent of her, and no matter what happened, he knew he couldn't lose her, even if she never saw him as more than a friend.

She pulled back and looked up at him. "I need to tell you something."

"It's fine, Gina, really."

"It's not. I need to tell you that you are your own amazing person who I have always loved to be around. Always--and that is still true. You are unique from your brother, you have your own qualities that I love and I just want you to know that."

"Thank you. And I want you to know that I will always be here for you and not through some sense of obligation. Me, Christian Andros, loves to be with you. End of story."

She stood on her tiptoes, kissed him on the cheek and gave him one of her brightest smiles. And he knew he could wait as long as he had to. And then she said something that made his heart melt.

"So where are you taking me on our next date?"

~

That date ended up being a trip to the mall and dinner nearby. She said it didn't need to be anything fancy as long as they were able to spend time together. She needed to get some items for the baptism that coming Sunday. Christian didn't care as long as he was with her. It was fun going from store to store crossing off all the items off her list. When they were seated at dinner, he decided to delve into awkward territory.

"How do you feel about Sunday?"

She looked at him with a raised eyebrow. "What do you mean?"

"Are you sad? Happy? Nervous?"

"All of the above. I'm trying not to think of the sad parts but then I tell myself I have to think of them or else all of it will hit me on Sunday and I will be a blubbering mess."

"You could never be a mess."

"Nice try."

"Will you tell me what you need? A hug, some space--just tell me what to do."

"Just be you, Chris, that's all I need."

"I will as long as you don't hide things from me. If

you miss Alex tell me, don't sugarcoat it to spare my feelings."

"I miss him every day."

"Me too."

"But you make every day a little easier."

"You, too."

~

The baptism could not have gone more perfectly. Everyone gave Gina the space—and yet the love and comfort—she desperately needed. It was all about baby Alex and it was amazing. Helena wanted to host a celebration at her home afterward and Gina didn't argue. The party was winding down and Gina found herself scanning the room looking for Christian as she hadn't spent much time with him today. She expected he kept his distance as he reasoned that the day was about Alex Jr. and his father—and he was right. The last thing Christian wanted to do was confuse her, but she looked his way and all he wanted was to go and be near her. He stood in the corner lost in his thoughts while she talked with her parents and Grace and everyone doted over his nephew.

"Are you going to talk to her today or what?" asked Anna as she came over.

"She's busy."

"She's been staring at you across the room all day."

"No, she hasn't."

"Okay, my mistake," and she walked away.

He continued to look her way, when Alex started crying and Gina said she needed to get him home and ready for bed. If her parents weren't there, he would have offered to go with her. He was dying to spend some time alone with her, but they would be gone in two days and he would take her out again then. She said goodbye to most everyone in the room then headed toward him and he couldn't move.

"Hey stranger, what have you been doing over here all alone?"

"Letting you enjoy your guests. I can see you any time."

"So, when will that next time be?"

"Tuesday?"

"It's a date."

He smiled widely, gave her and Alex a hug, and the whole room knew he was done for. And she wasn't far behind. Her head just needed to catch up with her heart.

Chapter 20

A month later, Gina and Elizabeth were on Gina's couch chowing down on salt and vinegar chips and watching The Wedding Planner, one of their favorite go to romantic comedies and Gina couldn't help but think this was what it was like when she started dating Alex. She and Elizabeth were college roommates and after her first date with him she couldn't wait to download it all to Elizabeth. The giggling, the laughter, the wondering what would happen next was all right there again.

"So has he kissed you yet?"

"No. I think he might be afraid. I'm thinking about kissing him."

"Really?"

"Yes. I was the one who said I needed time. I mean if I were him I wouldn't know what to think either."

"I think you should go for it. When do you see him again?"

"Tomorrow. We're watching a movie over here."

"Perfect. You better call me right after."

~

Christian arrived at Gina's the next day with snacks in tow, dropped them on the kitchen table after saying a quick hello to Gina and walked over to pick Alex up off the floor where he had been playing.

"My day was great thanks for asking."

He rushed over to her, put Alex back on the floor, and apologized. "I'm sorry it's just been a while since I've seen him."

"Yeah, yeah now I know where I stand."

"I have missed you."

"You saw me two days ago."

"It doesn't matter," he said inching closer until they were only a few inches apart, and suddenly Gina knew she wasn't going to have to make the first move. He leaned in and kissed her ever so gently and all she thought of was him. Then he hesitated and this time she moved in closer to kiss him again but he pulled away.

"What's wrong?"

He backed away, still not saying a word.

"Christian? What?"

"I'm sorry I can't. It's too weird."

"Umm. Okay."

He took her hand. "No, I mean the kiss was amazing but I can't. I can't be with my brother's wife."

"After all this time, you've been telling me how you wanted to be with me, how you had feelings for me, and now you want to go back. I don't think I can do that."

"I'm so sorry, Gina. I thought I could. But I can't," and he left her standing in the middle of the room, Alex now crying behind her and tears streaming down her face.

He got in his car and texted Elizabeth. "You need to go be with Gina," then he shut off his phone and drove away.

~

Gina finished telling Elizabeth what happened. Rather she got the story out in fits and starts between sobs. Ever the practical one, Elizabeth started with the bright side.

"Let's give Christian some credit. It took you awhile to see yourself with him. All you saw at first was his brother and then you got over it. He will too."

"But what if he doesn't? Everything is changed now. We can't go back. I can't go back. So now after everything I lost one of my best friends!"

Her crying started in earnest again and Elizabeth pulled her close repeating that it was going to be okay and praying that it would be.

~

Anna wondered why the heck Christian wasn't picking up his phone which was going straight to voicemail. He wasn't answering her texts either, and then her phone rang, and she saw it was her mother.

"Mom, have you heard from Christian?"

"No, that's why I am calling you. He won't respond to Dad or me."

"Same here. Let me call Gina. She probably knows. I will call you back."

Gina saw that Anna was calling and sent it to voicemail.

"Mom, Gina isn't picking up either. Something's going on."

"Can I come pick you up and we will go over

there."

"Yup. See you soon."

Helena hoped everything would be okay, especially since things were finally coming together. Her heart still ached for Alex and Teresa every day but they were all healing. The baby was definitely a big part of that as was having Gina back in their life. And the thought of Christian and Gina getting together was so exciting. Everything just had to be okay.

~

Christian heard the car pull up, saw his mother was with Anna, and knew he had to get it over with, so he opened the door then walked away without even saying hello.

"Whoa, what happened to you," said Anna, taking in his messy hair, scruffy face, sweats and wrinkled T-shirt.

"I've had a rough few days, and I really don't want to talk about it."

"Listen, Bro, you know it will be better if you just tell us and get it over with. Is it Gina?"

"We kissed. And all I thought of was how unhappy Alex would be with me, what people would think, so I told her it wouldn't work, and I left. We haven't talked since."

"Well, how do you even know she is okay, Christian?" Helena asked. "You know she has a history of depression. You can't just do that and leave her there."

"I didn't, I texted Elizabeth to check on her and I assumed she did. I turned my phone off after that."

"I'm calling Elizabeth," said Anna, turning away and leaving her mother to deal with him for now.

"Elizabeth, it's Gina. I just found out from Christian what happened the other night. Is Gina okay?"

"Not really. I'm sorry I wanted to call you but she didn't want to have you choose sides. She figured you would find out eventually."

"I'm going over there," said Anna. "Mom I think you should come with me."

"Let me know …"

But Helena just shut the door without answering her son. She knew he was in pain but right now her worries were with Gina. After everything that happened, she was not going to let her sink back into that pit of despair.

~

They knocked on the door and Gina immediately embraced both of them in a huge hug.

"Thank you for coming."

"We would have come earlier but we just found out what happened," said Anna.

"I didn't want to bother you but I desperately wanted to talk to you."

"Gina, we are here for you, and you know that," said Helena. "But I'm proud of you. It looks like you are doing okay."

"I am. I wallowed for at least a day but then I had a talk with God, and I refused to let myself sink back into that hole. And lucky for me the day after it happened, I had grief group and that really helped me heal. I am so thankful to God for having me find that group and having me finally open my heart to it."

"Yeah, I remember how you much you hated it there," said Anna. "And Grace."

"I know. We laugh about that now."

"My son is a mess if that makes you feel better."

"Not really, but thank you. I'm just so sad because I have lost one of my best friends."

Helena just sat holding Gina's hand. Her daughter-in-law wasn't ready to hear it yet but Christian and Gina were not done. She knew they were going to find their way back together.

~

A few weeks later Gina was out shopping as Grace had been dying to watch Alex and wanted to give Gina some time to herself. She still had several hours to kill as Grace gave her strict orders to not come back before five. And she told her not to eat as she would be preparing a meal for them and was inviting Anna and Elizabeth over to join them. Gina decided to go for coffee and read a book for the rest of her time alone. How long had it been since she had done that? She couldn't even remember back that far. She just had settled down with her novel when she heard a voice from the past.

"Gina Andros?"

"Tony Donelli?"

She stood up to embrace him then gestured for him to sit with her. "How long has it been?"

"Too long, Gina. And I'm so sorry about what happened to Alex and Teresa."

"I know thank you for sending the beautiful card. And tell your parents thank you as well."

"I will. I heard you had a baby."

"I did. He is usually with me but my friend insisted I take a day for myself today, so he is at home with her."

"You look amazing. I'm so glad I ran into you to

see that you are doing so well."

"I am. It's been awful to say the least but I have had friends and family there with me to get me through and I have come out on the other side. But, what are you doing in town? Are you visiting your parents?"

"I just moved back here."

Gina couldn't hide her surprise. She had met Tony years ago when she first moved to the area after Alex and she got engaged. They were both members of the same church and spent a lot of time together with the young adult's group who often took part in social activities, outside of their Bible studies and the things they did volunteering. She remembered Alex being jealous of him what with his dark Italian features, which he knew was Gina's type. Luckily, his own Greek features were pretty darn close.

"Why did you decide to come back?"

"My parents are getting older. I was getting tired of the city and a good job opportunity came up and I decided to take it. I look forward to connecting with everyone again. I was going to call Christian soon. How is he doing?"

"Good."

"Do you not stay in contact with the family anymore?"

"I do but not with Christian. I don't really want to get into it."

He wondered what the story was there. He couldn't imagine Christian was happy with that. He remembered how well they got along. Christian, Gina and Alex always spent a ton of time together.

"Listen, can I get your number? I would love to see you again and would love to meet your son."

"I would like that too."

He hugged her goodbye, telling her how nice it was to run into her and promised to contact her soon.

Gina walked in the door at 5:30 and was immediately met with quizzical looks.

"I'm so sorry! I ran into someone and lost track of time."

"That's fine," said Grace, "But these two were like mother hens wondering what had kept you. Come on let's sit down to eat and you can tell us about your day."

Alex was already in his highchair with Elizabeth doting over him while he stuffed his mouth with Cheerios.

"So, Gina, who did you run into today?

"Tony Donelli. He just moved back to town."

Elizabeth and Anna exchanged glances and Grace was dying to know the back story there and fortunately she didn't have to wait long.

"How long were you with him?"

"At least an hour. We just started talking and time flew by."

"Anyone care to fill me in on this guy?" asked Grace.

"We were friends when I first moved to the area. We spent a lot of time together in church activities. He knew Christian too as they went to high school together and were pretty friendly until Tony moved away for a job. In fact he told me he is going to call Christian."

Anna couldn't help but wonder what Christian would think of that, as her brother knew Tony had always liked Gina but could never do anything about it as she was engaged to Alex.

"Are you going to see him again?" Elizabeth asked.

"He said he is going to call me this week."

~

Tony texted Christian shortly after leaving Gina that day.

"Hey, man, guess who is back in town? Want to meet for a drink?"

Christian looked at the phone and couldn't stop smiling despite his foul mood. He had missed his friend and was eager to get out of the house and Gina off his mind.

"Are you free tonight?"

"Just tell me where and when."

~

They met two hours later at Nick's and spent the first hour talking non-stop, filling each other in on the highlights of the past few years.

"So I ran into Gina today."

Christian almost choked on his beer.

"She looks amazing."

"Dude, that's my brother's wife. Really?"

"Sorry, Chris. I just meant that it was great to see her looking so well after everything she has gone through. I have thought of her a lot over the past year or so and it was just really nice to see her."

"Yeah, she had a long road to healing but is doing so much better."

"She told me she hasn't talked to you in a while. Did something happen?"

"Why, what did she say?"

"Nothing. She said she didn't want to talk about it that's why I am asking you."

"I don't really want to talk about it either. It's just

been hard for all of us and I guess Gina and I are still working through some things."

"You aren't ..." he didn't know how to finish.

"No, nothing like that."

"Just wondering. I know you always had a special relationship with her."

"I did," was all he offered.

"So you won't mind if we got together again?"

"Why would I mind?"

"Just checking, Bro. You want another beer?"

"No, I'm good. Listen it was really nice catching up but I need to go," and he slapped a ten on the bar, gave his friend a quick slap on the back and walked out of there as fast as he could, and drove straight to Anna's. When she let him in she knew immediately something was wrong.

"Did you know Gina saw Tony and they are going to see each other again?"

"Yeah, I just found out today."

"Why didn't you tell me?"

"Well, first I just left there a few hours ago, and second, why would I think you wanted to know that. Have you changed your mind about dating her?"

"No."

"You can't have it both ways, Christian."

"I know," he said burying his face in his hands. "Does she like him?"

"Christian! They spent an hour together. I don't know. You know they always got along and that he always liked her. And I have to warn you Gina has been pretty lonely. I wouldn't be surprised if she fell for him. So if you are having second thoughts about your decision you should figure it out quick."

Of course, he was. But then he remembered how he felt after kissing Gina. All he felt was how disappointed Alex would be with him. He couldn't live with that. But he also didn't want her to be with anyone else.

~

Tony only waited two days before texting Gina asking if they could get together. He offered to come to the house so he could meet Alex and she immediately agreed. They decided on the next day and she was a little surprised at how excited she felt then it dawned on her that even with all the people in her life she was still lonely. She knew most of that was due to the void Christian had left, and she was smart enough to know that Tony couldn't fill that for her but it was nice to look forward to seeing someone again.

~

Tony showed up the next day with a homemade container of chocolate chip cookies.

"Do you still like these as much as you did all those years ago?" he said as he greeted her.

"Of course!" she said after giving him a quick hug.

He saw Alex on the floor and immediately went over to him and commented on how amazing he was.

"You know one of these days someone is going to walk in this house and greet me with as much emotion as they greet that little guy," she joked.

"I'm sorry," he said, immediately feeling bad.

"Relax, Tony I'm just kidding. And you are absolved as you brought me cookies."

~

When Tony left a few hours later she was surprised at how sad she felt to see him leave. It was like no time had passed since they last saw each other, and they talked non-stop filling each other in on what was going on in their lives. Before he left, he asked her if she would be open to going out to dinner with him and she immediately said yes.

~

The next day at grief group when the floor was open for whoever wanted to share, Gina raised her hand, and no one was surprised as this was pretty common now. They were all so proud of how far she had come. In fact, these days she often served as inspiration to new members of the group who had also suffered devastating loss.

"Yes, Gina," and Dr. Roberts noticed she looked more timid than normal.

"I feel weird asking but I have no one else to talk to about this who would understand. Can we talk about dating?"

Many people in the room who had already gone through that milestone smiled and Gina could tell they were ready to start sharing their wisdom.

"Do you care to be a little more specific, Gina?"

"Well, I started seeing someone a few months ago, just a few dates, and it didn't work out. But anyway, when that started I had a ton of guilt but then I finally overcame that but then the other person ended it. I don't really want to get into that. But now someone else from my past has come back into my life and we are going out on a date and I don't feel guilty. And that in itself makes me feel guilty. That makes no sense, right?"

Two people actually laughed out loud now.

"Gina, we are all so proud of how far you have come," said one woman in the group who had been there way before Gina arrived. "I think so many of us are jumping up and down on the inside for you. I know you thought you would never get there but look at you. You want to move forward and that is amazing. My advice for you is to go slow and listen to your heart."

Other people shared advice with Gina, and the conversation was helpful to many others in the room as well, but all Grace could think of was that Christian better get his act together quick. But she couldn't say anything. Once they became friends, she promised Gina she would never share anything from grief group with others—if Gina wanted to that was up to her. All she could do was pray that God would speak to Christian and that whatever was happening between Gina and Tony didn't progress quickly.

When Gina and Grace walked to their cars together after the group, in much more silence than normal, Gina asked if Grace would watch Alex on Friday night so she could go out with Tony. It was left unsaid that she didn't want the others to know about the date, which is why she asked Grace and not Elizabeth or Anna.

"Sure," was all she could manage before getting in her car and driving away.

~

Gina was now capable of getting ready on her own, thank goodness. She knew they were going for dinner but wasn't sure where, so she opted for a simple blue dress that always gained her compliments, then headed downstairs to wait for Grace and then Tony to show up.

Tony surprisingly arrived first as Grace was running a few minutes late. As soon as she opened the door, she was met by Tony holding a beautiful bouquet of flowers and she immediately broke into a huge smile.

"Wow, you look beautiful," he said, as he gave her

an admiring gaze. "These are for you."

"Thank you." She leaned over and kissed him on the cheek then gestured for him to come inside.

"Can I go see Alex now?" he joked, "Now that I have greeted you properly." She swatted him away playfully, and Alex immediately started crawling over to him with a huge grin on his face.

"Wow, I guess he remembers me."

"It seems he does," and Gina wondered why her stomach was doing flip flops that she couldn't control. She watched him playing with Alex and noticed how nice he looked in his khaki pants and white button-down shirt.

The doorbell rang and Gina let Grace in and introduced the two of them. She couldn't help but notice how Grace assessed him from head to toe, but didn't give away anything in her expression.

"It was very nice to meet you, Grace," Tony said as they left.

"You too, Tony. You guys have a great time."

Then Grace closed the door wondering why he couldn't have been ugly and impolite instead of the dashing Godly man that he seemed to be.

~

Tony chose an amazing seafood restaurant in the next town over and she wondered if he knew what a blessing that was for her. She wanted to reconnect with him without worrying about who they may run into at a restaurant in town. What looks she would get from people who may have seen her on a previous date with Christian. She knew she shouldn't care what others thought but that was easier said than done.

Dinner was amazing and she marveled once again at

how easy it was to be with him.

"So," she said, and just the way she said it alerted him something big was coming.

"How come you never settled down? I know when we spent all that time together, we always talked about how you wanted to start a family."

When he didn't answer right away, she started to apologize.

"Gina, stop, its fine," as he reached out and took her hand. "It's not like I have some big story. I just never found the right person. I wanted a Godly woman to share my life with and I just haven't found her yet."

When he said it he seemed to be staring right in her soul. "Maybe you will find someone like that here."

"I think maybe I will."

~

At the end of their date, Tony walked her to the door and drew her in for a hug.

"Thank you so much for a wonderful night, Gina. I don't want to scare you off but I would like to see you again."

She was surprised at how much she already wanted to set their next date as well.

"I drop Alex with the Andros' every Sunday for their family dinner so I have plenty of time then if you want to do something."

"That would be amazing. How do you feel about a hike?"

"I would love that. You and I were pretty good at that if I remember correctly."

"Great I will text you tomorrow. Sleep well."

And she knew that she would.

~

Helena and Gina had come to an agreement that Gina dropped Alex off on Sundays a little before Christian got there. She didn't need to be put in an awkward situation to which Helena was sympathetic and understood. But, for some reason this Sunday when she pulled up Christian had already arrived.

John answered the door, and she gave him all the necessary instructions, and said she would be by in several hours to pick him up. Then Christian followed her out.

"Gina, can you please stay for dinner. This is crazy that we can't be in the same room together."

"It's fine, Christian. I have plans today but thanks."

"Next week?"

"You know, I don't think so. I think we should just leave it alone."

I'm sure you like having time alone but if you ever change your mind let me know."

"Thanks."

"So, what are your plans today?"

"Christian, what are you doing?"

"What? I miss you Gina."

"Well, you were the one that ended things and I told you we can't go back."

"I was only making conversation."

"Fine, I'm going on a hike with Tony today. Is that what you wanted to hear?"

He didn't move and she knew she hurt him but he pushed her to it. She was almost to her car when he yelled out.

"Wow, that didn't take you long."

She spun around so fast she almost lost her balance. "Why are you doing this to me? You made this decision not me. I'm just trying to move on with my life. It's a hike, Chris, back off."

She drove away trembling and even though it was only a five-minute ride home she was full on shaking when she pulled in next to Tony who was in his car waiting for her to get back. She didn't know what to do so she just sat there trying to gain a composure that just wouldn't come. He got out of the car and knocked and when he saw her face full of tears he got in the car and held her. Gina wasn't sure how long they stayed like that but she wondered if Christian knew he literally sent her into another man's arms—something that wouldn't have happened if he wasn't so busy pushing her away.

She finally pulled away from Tony's embrace and apologized.

"What happened, Gina?"

She didn't want to tell him but the whole story came out.

"I thought he was acting odd that time I ran into him and I told him I saw you. It all makes sense now."

"But it doesn't. He has no reason for this to bother him."

A smile started to play on his lips.

"Gina, you are an amazing woman. Of course, it's going to bother him. Even if he can't be with you it doesn't mean he doesn't want to or is okay with you spending time with someone else. You know, that right?"

She was getting indignant now.

"Well, he can't just expect me to stay home and pine over him and not move on with my life."

"I'm glad to hear you say that. You still feel like going on that hike? You can work out some of your frustrations on the trails?"

"Heck, yes let's go."

~

Several hours later after Tony had dropped her off and she was leaving to go pick up Alex, she was happy she didn't stay home and sulk. She had so much fun with Tony who made her smile and laugh for most of the day. She only hoped that when she pulled up to the Andros' that Christian would be gone. She was relieved to see his car was no longer parked in the drive.

It was John once again who answered the door with Alex in his arms. Alex immediately reached out to Gina with his pudgy little arms as soon as he saw her.

"Gina, have you eaten?" asked Helena as she rounded the corner. She hadn't and was absolutely famished and knew Helena would have something way more delicious than anything in her fridge. She didn't want to get the third degree about her day but Helena's food was worth it so she settled in for what was to come.

After she had sufficiently stuffed herself and put back on any calories she had just burned off, Helena asked about her hike, something Gina never mentioned, proving that Christian definitely told them. Not that she was surprised.

"It was really fun. It was a beautiful day and nice to get out there and exercise."

"So what is Tony up to these days?" asked John.

She knew he was fishing as she was sure Christian told his father he met Tony for drinks but she played along.

"He was sick of big city life and got a good job here so moved back home."

Helena seemed to be thinking of her next move and finally came to the rescue of her son.

"You know Christian didn't mean to upset you Gina?"

"I know, but he did. And if he is jealous, first he is the one who ended it and second all he did was just push Tony into being there for me, something Christian could have done if this whole situation hadn't gotten so out of control."

"I just pray that he will come to his senses and that when he does it won't be too late."

"It just may be, Helena. Anyway, thank you for a wonderful meal but it's been a long day and I better get this guy home to bed."

"Alright, dear, love you."

"Love you too."

~

After she left it was John who expressed his frustration.

"I don't know what is wrong with our son. But he better figure it out quick before he loses his chance at so much happiness."

"John Andros, I didn't think you concerned yourself with such things."

"I usually don't but the whole world knows what a perfect match those two are. It's almost as if God has ordained it."

"Well, He may just be the only one who can make this work and get those two to see the light."

~

Christian lay on his couch, channel and social media surfing all at the same time and thinking of Gina. He stopped on a Facebook post of Tony's from today. It was a photo of him on the hike, beautiful scenery behind him with the words, "Thankful for the most wonderful day. God is good." Christian threw down his phone, trying to put all thoughts of those two behind him. But Gina was never far from his mind. Then he did something he rarely did—he prayed. Prayed that somehow God could lift this feeling of guilt he felt whenever he thought of Gina and him together. Prayed that if it was His will that they were together that God would take these awful feelings—feelings that Alex was staring down at him every day angrier than ever that Christian was trying to be with his wife.

~

Gina and Tony now had a standing date every Sunday, and often saw each other during the week as well. And they texted often and whenever she heard from him, he always put a smile on her face. But she missed her friends. They pulled back after she started seeing Tony—not because they didn't like him—it was really impossible not to. She imagined it was because they really wanted her to be with Christian, so it was awkward to be around her and talk about Tony. But she missed her girls—they were a huge part of the reason she was doing so well now. She sent off a group text to Grace, Anna and Elizabeth. "Please can we have a girl's night this week? I miss you!"

The yeses came in immediately.

~

The next day they were all gathered at Gina's talking a mile a minute, chowing down on chips, pretzels and chocolate. They were having a blast—though no awkward subjects came up—namely Christian or Tony.

"Alright can we talk about the elephant in the room?" asked Gina.

"Who are you calling an elephant," joked Grace. Gina threw a pillow at her.

"Come on, you guys know what I mean. We are having so much fun but I know you guys are avoiding talking about Tony or Christian because you don't want to upset me. I want you to be yourself around me."

Grace needed no further prodding.

"Gina, we just want you to be happy."

"And Gina, Chris is my brother. Obviously, I'm a little biased here so that is why I have stayed out of this. I don't want to sway your feelings one way or the other."

"So, give us the skinny, Gina," said Elizabeth. "All of it."

She lit up like a birthday cake. "Tony makes me so happy. He is easy to be around. We have all the same interests and faith in God. I feel comfortable around him."

"Is there a spark?"

"There is. But, we haven't kissed yet."

All the girls showed their surprise.

"I know, I was a little surprised too but I think he wants to go slow with me. And I haven't said anything but I think he knows I have some feelings for Christian, so he doesn't know what to do with that."

"So, you do have feelings for my brother still?"

"Of course, I do, Anna. Those don't just go away. But I wish I didn't. He told me how he felt. It's not going anywhere so I need to find happiness elsewhere. And Tony does make me happy. And I get butterflies when I'm around him too."

They all noticed that now Gina looked upset.

"See, Gina this is why we didn't bring any of this up. We want you to be happy and now you just look sad."

"I am when we talk about Christian. We were best friends. Imagine what you feel like when you lose your best friend. I miss him. But I just can't go back. It's too weird. I wish we just always stayed as friends because then everything would just be normal now. I could move forward with Tony, Christian wouldn't care and all would be great."

"Have you prayed about all this?" asked Grace.

"I have. I have prayed that Christian changes his mind but clearly that's not happening."

"But have you asked God if Tony is the one for you?"

"I guess, I haven't."

"Well, Gina, you know that God has a plan."

"I do. I just really wish he would tell me what it is."

"Don't we all," said Grace. "You know that when it's the right time he will reveal it to you."

~

The next day, Tony surprised Gina by showing up at her door with a dozen roses. She smiled immediately when she saw him.

"What's the occasion?"

"I just missed you and wanted to see you. Is that okay?"

"Of course! I am glad you came. Come on, let's sit."

"Where's the little guy?"

"We had a big day, and he was exhausted, so I just put him down."

He sat next to her on the couch with only a few inches of space between them. "Gina, there is another reason I came over tonight. There is something I can't stop thinking about."

"What is it?"

"This," then he leaned in, placed his hand on her face and kissed her gently but with meaning. When he pulled back, she immediately heard a clear voice in her ear, "He is not the one I have chosen for you." She couldn't help but thinking the one she wanted didn't want her back.

"Gina, what's wrong? I am so sorry. I shouldn't have done that. I just felt like maybe it would be okay."

"It is okay. I have been waiting for you to do that."

"You have? Then why do you look so sad?"

She knew Tony for years and always felt completely comfortable around him, and they had the same faith, so she lay it out there. "I just felt God speak to me. It was so clear."

"I'm afraid to ask what he said."

"I'm sorry," was all she could say.

"I am too, Gina. I just hope whoever God has destined for you is smart enough to realize it—and wise enough to be still and listen for God to speak to him."

"You know you are amazing right? And that you are going to find the most wonderful woman of God to spend your life with."

"I know."

"Do you think we could still be friends?"

"Maybe. But not right now, Gina. I'm sorry but I have really strong feelings for you and it's just too hard."

Then Gina watched a second friend walk out her

door, probably forever.

The next day was Sunday dinner and Gina really didn't want to drop Alex off and be alone. She missed her family and wanted to be with them.

So she showed up right on time—not 30 minutes early as she always did so she could avoid Christian. "Gina, I was beginning to worry about you," said Helena, then she tried to speak telepathically to Gina wondering why she came now when Christian was here.

"Hi Gina," said Christian, as he walked into the room. "Can I take this little guy from you. I missed him so much."

"Sure."

"Gina, let me take these things from you so you can go enjoy your day," said Helena.

"Actually," she said shyly. "I was wondering if I could stay."

Anna and John were all in the room now and their faces lit up.

"Of course, you can. Anna set another place at the table."

~

For the next month, things slowly went back to normal on Sundays at the Andros' house. Christian and Gina started to talk to each other again—it was difficult not to when she was there for hours—having dinner then playing games together with the family as was the tradition. Christian wondered what happened with Gina and Tony. Anna told him they were no longer together but she offered no further details and he wondered if Gina had even shared those with Anna.

Alex was a year now and running all over the place

and kept everyone on their toes. She could tell he was particularly fond of Christian. They were outside right now playing in the backyard and she sat at the window and watched them, a scene that did not escape Helena and John who cast knowing looks at each other. There may just be hope yet.

Gina was home later that night getting ready to put Alex to bed. As was their tradition, every night she sat with him on the rocker and showed him the photo of his Dad. "That's your Dada." Can you say Dada?"

He was already calling her Mama and she wanted to be sure he knew about his amazing father who he shared his name with.

"Dada."

She about dropped the photo on the floor and tears immediately sprang to her eyes.

~

Elizabeth sent a group text to Grace and Anna and at the last minute added Christian to the chain. Gina's birthday was the next week and she felt like they should do something special for her. Her last birthday was pretty awful, and her friend wanted this one to be special.

"Can we all take Gina out next week for her birthday? The girls plus Christian LOL."

"Sounds great," said Elizabeth.

"I'm there," said Grace.

"At Vinny's?" asked Christian.

"Sounds great," Elizabeth texted back. Can one of you ask your Mom to watch Alex?"

"Yes," said Anna, "Though I know Mom will want to invite us all back there for cake."

"Sounds perfect," they all replied.

The following Thursday on Gina's birthday she was about to walk out the door with Alex to drop him off at Helena's and meet Anna there, when someone rang the doorbell.

"Christian? What are you doing here?" she asked.

"Well, first of all you should get the full treatment on your birthday, so I was going to drive you and Alex over to my Mom's."

"Sounds good, but I feel like there is more to the story."

"I was invited to come along tonight, and I wanted to check with you first to make sure that was okay. I don't want to ruin your birthday."

"Of course, I want you to come, Chris."

That was the first time she called him that since ...

"I have missed my best friend. I am glad things are getting back to normal with us."

"Me too. It's your birthday but I feel like I am the one who was just given a gift," he told her and she knew he was holding back tears, and she couldn't help but wonder why that was the case.

~

They had the most amazing time together and now they were all back at Helena's and just finished off a delicious chocolate cake she had made for her.

"Thank you all so much for giving me such a special birthday, but I think I should get this guy home," she said as she walked over to take him out of Christian's arms where he was laying peacefully.

Alex immediately started crying, looked up at Christian and said, "Dada."

Nobody moved or knew what to say. It seemed like minutes passed before Gina awkwardly said her goodbyes and went to rush out the door.

"Gina, wait," said Christian. "You don't have a car. I have to drive you home."

Knowing she needed to be rescued, John jumped in.

"I'll take her," he said.

When they pulled up to her house John helped her bring everything inside while she carried Alex and his car seat.

"Thank you, John, do you mind letting yourself out while I go put Alex to bed."

"Of course."

She was downstairs not even five minutes later and was startled to see John still there. He could tell she had been crying and she quickly tried to hide the stains that she knew were on her face.

"Gina, are you okay?"

She immediately burst into tears again and John held her and let her cry some more.

~

He went back to the house and wasn't surprised to see his son still there.

"How is she, Dad?"

"Well, she cried a lot but we didn't really talk about it."

"Why didn't you?"

"What was I going to say, Christian?" said John in frustration. "Her heart is breaking."

And while neither said it his parents both looked at him like it was his fault.

Christian thought about Gina every minute since that day he kissed her and then rejected her. He didn't feel any less love toward her, but the feelings of guilt were still there. He wanted them to go away but didn't know how to make that happen. He had been praying more frequently now and with more intensity that God would help him through this situation. It helped but he still didn't know what to do. Was he supposed to try to kiss her again and just hope that he didn't see Alex's face of disappointment? He knew that wasn't the answer. He also couldn't help but wonder what happened between her and Tony. Maybe she decided she didn't want to be with anyone. As luck would have it, or maybe God planned it, he ran into Tony the next day while they were both running into Wawa after getting gas.

When Christian spotted him, it looked like Tony wanted to pretend he didn't see him.

"Tony."

"Hey, Christian."

"I thought maybe you would have texted me so we could get together again for a beer."

"Really?"

"Why not, I thought we were friends."

"Don't you think that would be awkward?"

"Why, because you dated Gina? Listen I don't know what happened with the two of you but it has nothing to do with me."

"Dude, you are so clueless. It had everything to do with you." And then he walked away.

Christian immediately texted Anna. "You have to find out what happened between Tony and Gina. I have to know sis."

"I'm not getting in the middle of this. You want to know you ask her. You guys need to clear the air about the other night anyway."

"What do you mean?"

"Christian, sometimes you are just a big dummy. Alex called you Dada. Seriously, don't you think you two need to figure that out?"

"You really did get all the brains in the family."

He decided to stop at Gina's as there was no way she would agree to see him if he texted first.

~

He showed up at eight when he knew Alex would be sleeping or close to it. When she saw him through the window, she wished she could ignore him but they may as well get this over with. Instinctively she ran her hands through her hair and straightened her outfit before answering.

"Hey, Gina."

"Hey, Christian. What's up?"

"Is Alex sleeping?"

"He is."

"Great, because we really need to talk."

She stood in silence and he knew she wasn't going to make this easy for him.

"Can we sit?"

"Sure," she said reluctantly before sitting on the far end of the couch. Christian took the spot next to her which he could immediately tell made her uncomfortable but he needed to be near her.

"So, the other day?"

"Yeah."

"What are we going to do?"

"I don't know, Christian. I guess if he keeps doing that, I just need to keep correcting him that you are his Uncle."

"Do you think that will work?"

She stood up from the couch, clearly uncomfortable

with the situation.

"What do you want me to do?"

"Gina, you and I have finally been finding our way back to being friends. I don't want this to ruin it and make us uncomfortable around each other again."

"I'm not the one who started that."

"Yes, I know you keep reminding me."

"You know what, you should just leave."

He knew he botched it badly but he listened to her and walked away—again.

He drove right to his sister's and spilled the story.

"Anna, you have to find out why they broke up."

"Christian, you have to stop being so obsessed. I don't see how it's going to change anything. And I'm your sister. I'm not the one to get this story out of her."

"Text Grace."

"Christian, back off. You ended it with her, and you need to leave it alone unless your feelings of guilt have gone away."

"They haven't."

"Then you need to let her go."

Chapter 21

Monday at grief group the meeting was about to start when Dr. Roberts motioned to someone who had just walked in. She gestured for them to come and take the empty seat next to Grace, two seats away from Gina—it was Christian.

Gina didn't think she had ever been so mad in her life. Why was he doing this to her? She knew deep down he cared for her but his feelings of devotion to his brother wouldn't allow him to pursue a relationship with her. As hard as that was she actually understood that. But then why was he here? Why was he constantly badgering her refusing to let her move on?

Grace took Gina's hand and gave it a squeeze. After the opening prayer Dr. Roberts gave the introduction into that night's session. It was about forgiveness, letting go of guilt, along with other's expectations of you.

Why were these messages always so spot on, but Gina already knew the answer.

"Gina, I want to talk about something you shared with the group last week—about hearing the voice of God. Are you okay with me telling that story as it ties into what we are talking about today?"

She couldn't breathe, and Grace gave her hand a squeeze again and whispered in her ear, "Gina, maybe this is meant to be. Why else would he have showed up tonight of all nights? Maybe you need to get it out in the open?"

She nodded.

"Do you want to share it?"

"I can't."

Noting the tension in the room, Dr. Roberts continued for Gina.

"Some of you weren't here last week so I will give you a quick recap. Gina was dating someone she felt really close to, someone who treated her like the amazing woman that she is, who she had feelings for, but God clearly spoke to her telling her essentially he wasn't part of God's plan for her."

"How do you think that made her feel? How would that make us feel?"

"I think it's rare that things in our life are going great, when we are happy, and God tells us that's not His plan for us. I can't even imagine how Gina felt at that point," said a woman in the room.

"I think she probably felt betrayed by God. She lost her husband, her daughter, for a while, her family, and now that she was finding happiness, she felt like God was taking that away," said a man who had lost his wife a year or so ago.

"So, what can we do in these situations? How can we still listen to the voice of God?"

Gina spoke up now, her anger still boiling within her. "We can pray, and we can continue to listen. But it's impossible when others are constantly in our face refusing to let us move on. Refusing to let us heal. Who continue to hurt us by not giving us space."

She was in tears now, so she grabbed her purse and ran out of the room. The discussion continued for another 15 minutes and before the meeting ended, Dr. Roberts turned to Christian and said, "Do you mind if I ask you why you came tonight?"

"I know now it was a big mistake and that I'm not making things easier for her. I'm so sorry," then he strode from the room as well, wondering why he kept making things worse.

Even though it was raining, Gina was waiting for him at his car, tears still streaming down her face which was red with anger, and he was shocked to see her.

"Gina, you are soaking wet."

She ignored him. "If I tell you what happened will you leave me alone? Is that why you came here tonight? To find out the details that transpired between Tony and me? To somehow listen in on my deep dark secrets? This is my place of solace, Christian. The place I heal— because every day of my life I am still healing. Why are you doing this to me?"

"I'm sorry. I'm so sorry. I shouldn't have come here. Please forgive me."

"I'm going to tell you what happened and then you need to leave me alone. It's simple. Tony kissed me. It was a great kiss, Christian, and I really was falling for him. I was happy with him, and he was making me forget all my feelings for you. Then you know what God said in my ear. 'He is not the one I have chosen for you.'"

Christian didn't know what to say. Now he was mad at God. He had been praying for guidance to help him through these feelings of guilt so he could be with Gina—so he could be happy, but that hadn't happened. Yet, there He was telling Gina Tony wasn't the one He chose for her. Was he the one? If yes, why was God not speaking to Christian? Why was He keeping them from being together? Why was he consumed by guilt regarding his feelings for Gina? About the fact that Alex Jr. called him Dada?

"You have nothing to say? Really, Chris?"

Maybe God was speaking to him since that time a few months ago when he kissed Gina. Maybe he just wasn't listening. So, he stepped toward her, pulled her in his arms and pressed his lips to hers, but she fought it, she wasn't going to let him hurt her again. She pulled away, looked him in the eye, then got in her car and drove away. Christian savored the kiss, and his feelings of guilt were gone. But he had a feeling it was now too late. He just stood in the rain and watched her leave.

~

When Gina walked in the door, Anna already knew what happened in the group that night with her idiot brother. Grace called her to give her the low down thinking Anna should know the state Gina would be in. Anna took one look at her, pulled her in her arms, and told her she was so sorry, and that it was going to be okay but wondering if it ever would be.

Gina really needed to talk to her friend, even if she was Christian's sister.

"So obviously you know what happened at group tonight but I need to tell you what happened with

Christian and me at the car."

She recounted her story, sobbing through it, and Anna's heart went out to her.

"Do you think he had a change of heart and that is why he kissed you again?"

"I don't know. But I love him, Anna. I pulled away but the kiss felt right. I always feel happy when I am in his arms. But that's why I need to stay away from him. Until he figures out how he feels and stops playing these games, Alex and I can't be around him. I realized tonight that I also need to protect my son."

~

Anna arrived at home that night and Christian was sitting on her porch waiting for her.

"Christian, I love you but you are killing me."

"How is she?"

"She loves you."

If he wasn't sitting down, he would have lost his balance. She loves him. And when he kissed her, he felt no feelings of regret, no feelings of betrayal toward his brother. A smile formed on his face, which left Anna wondering what had just happened.

"She loves me, Anna. And I love her. God has finally brought us to each other free of our baggage."

He was standing now so full of excitement for what was to come.

"Sis, you have to help me with my plan."

~

Five days later Anna and Christian had put everything into motion.

"I'm really glad this is happening tonight, Chris, because I am worried about Gina. You haven't contacted her since the kiss so now she thinks it's over for good. She's pretty sad, and I'm scared she might not even show up for Sunday dinner."

Christian had thought about that too. But he texted her this week saying he didn't want her to stop seeing the family and they would just have to figure out a way to make it work to which she agreed. He and his sister went over the details for tomorrow one last time and Christian knew he wouldn't be able to sleep tonight. Tomorrow couldn't come soon enough.

~

Gina pulled in the driveway and wondered why John, Anna and Helena were sitting on the porch. As soon as she pulled in they all descended on the car with a stroller, telling Gina they wanted to take Alex to the park down the road.

"Christian is waiting for you inside," said Helena. "We'll be back soon."

Wondering what had just happened she walked up to the door, and before she could knock Christian opened it for her. The sight of him took her breath away. He was wearing dark slacks, and a white tailored shirt and she noticed a cross around his neck, something she never saw on him before. She immediately felt underdressed in her capris pants and cotton top. At least she had spent time on the rest of her appearance— something she always did when there was even a chance she would see him.

She instinctively ran her hand through her hair, and he took her hand without saying a word. She looked around the living room which was full of candles and a few fresh bouquets of daisies.

"Christian, what's going on?"

He took both her hands in his and pulled her close,

so they were only a few inches apart.

"I love you, Gina. I'm so sorry for all I have put you through."

"Christian, you don't have to ..."

"Please, there is a lot I need to tell you. I wanted to be with you—all this time I wanted that more than anything. But at the same time, I felt such guilt that I couldn't shake. But last week when I kissed you it was different—all I thought of was you and me. And it's all I could think of since then. God brought me to you, Gina. I know that with all my heart. I have been praying this whole time and now I know that I also had healing to do I just feel awful that I hurt you in the process."

He looked at the tears streaming down her face and prayed they were tears of joy. She reached out to him and pulled him in for a tight embrace. She buried her face in his chest taking in the smell of him and only thinking of the two of them and the future they might have.

He pulled back so he could look at her, the questioning evident in his blue eyes.

"Is it too late?"

She put her hand to his cheek and gave her answer in a long, slow kiss full of promises.

"When will your parents be home? I assume they were all in on this."

"Not for a while, because we aren't done yet."

"Oh?"

They were still standing in front of each other when he dropped to one knee and Gina gasped in surprise.

"Gina, I've loved you since I met you all those years ago. That love of friendship has now turned into more. You have brought so much into my life, you, your son, and most importantly you brought me a strong faith in God. I can't wait anymore. I know without a doubt that you and I were meant to be together."

He pulled out a small box from his pocket and opened the most exquisite ring—one she had seen before. She knew it was Helena's mother's engagement ring, which she told Helena to give to Christian, the first born, for when he proposed. Gina immediately thought the ring was a sign that Helena had accepted her into the family once again—and that this time it would be forever.

"Will you marry me?"

Tears covered her face once again, and while he waited for an answer, he thanked the Lord for blessing him with such a beautiful woman who was also his best friend.

"Gina?"

"Yes."

"Yes, you will marry me?"

"Yes, Chris, I will marry you."

Now it was time for his tears to fall. She wiped them away then pulled him in for a tender kiss and immediately heard a single, clear voice. "He is the one I chose for you."

They were interrupted by a small knock. "Let's go tell them the news."

They both opened the door and their smiling faces and hands intertwined told the family all they needed to know.

~

One month later, Elizabeth, Anna, Helena and Maria took one look at Gina in her wedding dress and the tears were already flowing.

"Hey, how are we going to get through today if you girls can't stop crying?"

"We can't help it, Gina," said her mother. "We are just so happy for you. I can't imagine a couple that deserves this more than you two, two people who have gone through so much and now happiness instead of heartbreak lies in front of them."

"Thank you, Mom. I couldn't have done it without all of you."

"Are you ready?" Elizabeth asked.

"I am. I will see you out there."

Christian and Gina decided to have no attendants. This was a simple service, there were only 20 people here today gathered in the Andros' backyard. The sole member of the wedding party was Alex who would be standing at the front of the church next to Christian, as their official ring bearer.

Her family had left to take their seats and her father walked in the room as it was almost time to walk her down the aisle, and his eyes filled with tears.

"What is it with everyone crying today?" joked Gina.

"Gina, you have no idea how much your mother and I worried about you. But you are so strong, and you came through this, you kept your faith in God, and he rewarded you with an amazing man."

She smiled and looped her arm though his and they walked out of the back door and started down the makeshift aisle that was created between the two small rows of chairs. Christian gasped when he saw her, and felt as if everyone must have heard. She looked so beautiful in her simple sleeveless dress. A white beaded headband held her upswept hair in place which she was wearing in a style he loved so much. He loved to be able to see all her beautiful features on display.

She looked at him and smiled and wasn't surprised at how handsome he looked—but wondered how she got so lucky. She couldn't wait to reach him at the altar and join her hands in his. When she had almost reached him, Alex yelled "Mama," and ran down the aisle to give her a big hug. She didn't think she would cry that early but that did her in—his pure joy.

Gina took her place beside Christian and he took both her hands in his and they couldn't take their eyes off each other as her pastor started their ceremony. Then it came time for their vows which they had written for each other.

"Chris," she started. "You are my best friend and now I will also be able to call you my husband. You helped bring me out of the depths of grief and helped me find love again. Our story wasn't without challenges, but God was part of it from the beginning and He led us here today. I thank him every day for leading me to you. I will love you forever."

She stopped to wipe her eyes as did Christian, and many of the witnesses, but the couple wasn't done yet.

"Gina, we were friends from the first day I met you. All of our friends and family here today know the circumstances that brought us together—how we helped each other heal and go through a bit of hurt in the process. But I promise I will never hurt you again. I think of starting this life with you and Alex and it literally brings me to my knees. God is the one who brought us together and he will be at the center of this marriage. I can't wait to begin my life with you, to cherish you every day of my life and to treat you like the amazing woman and mother that you are."

She had to stop to dry her eyes once again. Then it was time to exchange rings and Christian thought nothing would ever compare to this, but only God knew of the million more amazing ones to come.

When the pastor pronounced them husband and wife neither of them waited for permission to kiss and the guests laughed while they met for a tender kiss and embrace.

~

After all the guests had left, the couple was at Gina's where, for now, they would make their home. Alex was at his Aunt Anna's for the night, so the two had the whole night together before they came together tomorrow to live as a family.

She had gone upstairs, and Christian followed behind her without her knowledge. He came up behind her, wrapped his hands around her waist and nestled his head on her shoulder.

"That."

He turned her slightly and looked at her quizzically.

"You can do that forever. That's what makes me feel safe and secure. It's what I dreamed of when we were apart. You know, when you were being a fool and not wanting to be with me."

He laughed but then turned her around fully to face him.

"I will love you forever and protect you and our family always."

"Family?"

"Yes, family, we don't want Alex to be all alone, do we? How amazing would it be to have a daughter who looks exactly like you, or a son that looks like his handsome father?"

She swatted him away playfully.

"You will have three children."

She pulled away from him.

"Gina, what's wrong? I'm sorry. I didn't mean to scare you but I thought we talked about having kids. I'm sorry we can go slow."

She was crying now and he couldn't believe he was screwing this up already.

"That's not why I am crying. God just spoke to me about our children."

"He did?"

"How do you feel about three?"

"I think we better go get started."

She smiled and pulled him into her arms once again, thinking of only him and their life together and how lucky she was to have come through the abyss and into his loving arms.

Go to http://www.tarataffera.com to sign up for my newsletter

Want to learn more about the Andros family? Look for book 2 in a Divine Love Series coming soon to hear Anna's story, and her search for love.

Read on to read the first chapter of book two in a Divine Love Series.

Anna looked at the friends and family gathered around her mother's patio, and was filled with pure joy. So why was she sad? What was that hole she felt in her heart, despite the love that surrounded her?

She looked over at her brother Christian and his wife Gina, who also happened to be Anna's best friend in addition to her sister-in-law. Those two were the picture-perfect postcard of happiness. And she wasn't jealous. How could she be when she knew of the grief they both went through—that she went through when her brother Alex died, Gina's first husband. The horrific car accident that claimed his life, and her niece Teresa, took years for them to all get over. But, in the end it brought Gina and Christian together.

Alex Jr. interrupted Anna's thoughts when he came running over. "Aunt Anna, look. Look at what Nana Helena gave me."

"Are those bubbles?" Oh I love bubbles. Did you know your Dad and I used to blow those together when we were little?"

"You did?"

"Yup, and we would chase them all over the yard."

"Will you do that with me, Aunt Anna?"

"I promise. Let's do it a little later okay?"

He flashed that huge smile that always reminded her of her older brother, and took off to the man he called Dad, his Uncle Christian. But he really was his Dad. One day when he was old enough, Gina and Christian planned to tell him that Alex died when Alex Jr., was already in her womb—though she didn't know it at the time.

"Dad, Aunt Anna said when you guys were little you used to chase bubbles around."

Christian looked over at Anna and gave her a knowing wink, knowing that was his brother and sister's thing, though Christian would join in from time to time.

"We did, buddy."

"She said she will blow bubbles with me later and we can chase them. Do you want to do it with us?"

"You bet I do."

Alex's attention turned quickly to his mom and new baby sister, Evangeline, Eva, as they all affectionately called her. Alex was three now, and the kid never stopped smiling, especially when he was around the baby.

Anna watched the four of them all huddled together. Though no one else would likely notice, despite the smile on his face, Anna could see the worry that resided there as Christian looked down at his wife and whispered in her ear. She would bet money that Christian just asked his wife if she was okay, as Anna could tell just by the slight nod of Gina's head. This was Gina's first big family gathering since Eva was born. She battled post-partum depression with Eva, as she did with her first-born Teresa, and Christian worried about her incessantly.

"Hey, Anna, you look lost in thought. Making sure your brother doesn't hover over his wife all day?"

"Someone has to make sure he doesn't screw this up," she joked to her friend Elizabeth.

"Seriously, though, do you think she's okay?"

"I do, we just have to make sure she is surrounded by the people she loves and we help her out when she needs it. With Christian back to work, a new baby and Alex running around, it's got to be stressful."

"Well that's one of the reasons I came over here. I'm planning a girl's night at my house on Friday night with the three of us. You in?"

"Of course! We need one of these so bad."

"I know, we haven't had one since Eva was born. So bring on the junk food and the gossip."

Anna was feeling better already.

~

"Girls, I missed this so much," said Anna, as she dug her hand into the bowl of salt and vinegar chips.

"You! Oh my gosh, I have been dreaming of this," said Gina. "Well, maybe not dreaming since I hardly sleep anymore so how can I dream?"

Elizabeth and Anna looked at her—their faces etched with worry lines, even though they were way too young for those to have appeared.

"Stop looking at me like that you two. I'm fine. It was a joke."

"I know, Gina, we just worry about you," said Elizabeth.

"I know, and I love you guys for it, but really I'm okay. Come on this is supposed to be a girl's night. I don't get out much, tell me what's going on with you two."

"Anna had a date the other night," Elizabeth blurted out.

"What? Why am I just now hearing about this?"

"Because it wasn't a great date."

"So what, I still want all the gory details. Spill," Gina demanded.

"There is nothing to spill. It was boring, just like the date before that and the date before that."

Gina and Elizabeth exchanged glances.

"What?"

"Nothing," said Elizabeth.

Anna threw a pillow at her.

"Listen, you guys, it's no picnic out there."

"Gee, I wouldn't know anything about that, would I?" said Elizabeth. "Oh wait, I do. I haven't had a great date in forever either. Join the club, sister."

Now it was Gina looking over with a knowing glance and the hint of a smile.

"What?" the other two both said in unison.

"Nothing."

They raised their eyebrows at her.

"Fine. You know what I'm going to say."

"God has a plan," said Elizabeth.

"So you keep telling us," said Anna. "I just wish he would fill me in on what it is."

"Come on. Grace and I keep telling you two, the right man is out there waiting for you."

"We know. So you say," said Elizabeth, playfully. "And speaking of Grace, do you guys know why she couldn't be here tonight?"

"No, I was just going to ask you that," said Gina.

"She has a date."

"Good for her," said Anna, I hope it's better than mine.

Grace is old enough to be their mother, but they all became really close a few years ago when Gina met her in her grief group after Alex and Teresa died. Grace's daughter died in a brutal murder and her husband and Grace divorced sometime later. While Grace went to the group to heal, her husband retreated into himself and the walls he put up were too hard for Grace to knock down. She was devastated when he dropped the divorce papers on the table one day. That was a few years ago and this was just one of only a handful times she had gone out with another man.

"Well, she is coming over tomorrow to help me out with the kids," said Gina. "So I will get the full scoop."

"Great, while you are at it, get a date from her for another girl's night next week," said Anna.

"Perfect," said Gina. "I'll just be the old boring married woman and you three can fill me in your exciting dating lives."

Anna and Elizabeth both threw a pillow at her, and they all doubled over in laughter.

Author Bio

Tara Taffera is a journalist living in Stafford, Va., with her husband of 23 years, and her three daughters. In 2020, she realized her dream of writing her first novel, Love Ordained. She has always loved to read, and anyone who knows her knows how fast she can plow through a good book. Her mother always says, how as a youngster, she was always asking to go back to the library for more books. She started writing Love Ordained more than 20 years ago, and she finally made it a priority in early 2020, and finished the book—a Christian romance.

Social Media

https://www.facebook.com/authortarataffera
https://twitter.com/TaraTaffera
https://www.instagram.com/tarataffera/
https://www.linkedin.com/in/tara-taffera-b092545/
https://www.goodreads.com/author/show/21190784.Tara_Taffera
https://www.pinterest.com/ttaffera/

Made in the USA
Monee, IL
20 February 2021

61003550R00154